# Into the Realm of the Faeries

## Quest for the Staff of Enchantment

A Novel Written by M. J. Baxter

Order this book online at www.trafford.com
or email orders@trafford.com

Most Trafford titles are also available at major online book retailers.

Note for Librarians: A cataloguing record for this book is available from Library
and Archives Canada at www.collectionscanada.ca/amicus/index-e.html

Printed in Victoria, BC, Canada.

ISBN: 978-1-4269-2056-1 (sc)

*Our mission is to efficiently provide the world's finest, most comprehensive book publishing
service, enabling every author to experience success. To find out how to publish your book, your
way, and have it available worldwide, visit us online at www.trafford.com*

*Trafford rev. 11/24/2009*

 www.trafford.com

**North America & international**
toll-free: 1 888 232 4444 (USA & Canada)
phone: 250 383 6864 ♦ fax: 812 355 4082

## Dedication

So many people helped me create this
dream that I could fill a whole book with
their names, so I am going dedicate this
book to all who helped me make the movie
in the summer of eleventh grade. You know
who you are!

# Contents

# Prologue

In the beginning, the Faeries were the most powerful creatures that walked the earth, especially the males. There was one Faerie who was more memorable than the rest his name was Argus. Argus held the power of persuasion, so nobody questioned him. He fell in love with one of the most beautiful faeries in the realm her name was Bethany. His love was in vain however for Bethany's heart belonged to another—not even his persuasion could talk her out of that. Bethany would not speak the name to which her heart belonged, so Argus took matters into his own hands. One by one, the male population seemed to disappear until only Argus remained. He comforted the weeping faerie and bided his time until she might fall in love again—with or without his help.

After the disappearance of all the male faeries Argus declared himself, King and his subjects loved him. Bethany was by his side as Queen and they had five children. Three daughters named Charity, Destiny, and Evangaline; and two sons named Fernandez and Goodwin. The boys grew up peacefully until they reached ten and one half years exactly.

Then the fight for the crown began. Fernandez and Goodwin pulled the entire population into the war between them. Each boy had followers who thought he had more right to the crown and when Goodwin succeeded in taking it, he became King.

Goodwin's first act as King was to banish his brother and all of his followers from the Realm of the Faeries. One by one Fernandez and his subjects had their wings clipped and their memories erased so that they might never find their way back. Thus became the age of Humans. After the war, Goodwin heard rumors about a group of Faeries who had predicted this a few years before Argus had become King. He sought them out and decided to appoint them as the Ancestral Order and Argus joined them. They predicted that one more occurrence would happen where two sons born of the same father would destroy the world, as they knew it. Goodwin's second act as King was to gather a group of powerful faeries to prevent himself or any other King from ever rearing more than one son--at all costs, this prediction could never come true. This soon presented a problem to the Faeries however; their kind would not continue to grow as it had before Argus had appointed himself King. King Goodwin joined the Ancestral Order as he passed his throne to his son Hatch and left the problem for him to deal with.

By this time, King Hatch decided to send his father's advisors out into the world to locate those Faeries who were thrown out so many years ago. The advisors came back with news that the ex-faeries were indeed thriving. However, they had aged and some had ceased to exist. King Hatch assembled another team to study them. To study their ways and customs and to bring him back answers as to why they were no longer immortal. He would not hear from his team again until he too joined the Ancestral Order and passed his crown to his son Ira.

Argus, Goodwin, Hatch, and King Ira listened to how the outsiders were born, grew at a slower rate, and eventually died. However, there was no plausible reason as to why they were no longer immortal. King Ira decided that their research must continue until they knew why. Every seven years they decided they would take Human babies and replace them with a changeling—a magical creature created for the purpose of duplicating the baby that was taken and was programmed to eventually die—for research. However if the parents discovered the changeling and disposed of it properly their child would be returned. Mean while their race was idling. The Humans were close enough in looks, and were descendants of the Faeries too, so King Ira made another decision.

All the Faeries would mate with the Humans. However to make sure none of them ever got back into the Realm, their memories would be erased and they would be moved to a different part of the world. Time passed, many Faerie babies were born, they were all beautiful, and the population was booming again. Until the seventh year after the Human-Mating Law had passed. All the boys born from the Human-Mating Law, having reached seven years exactly began to show evil tendencies and kill their mothers. They then began to form groups and cause chaos everywhere they went. It was a storm of the Palace and the murder of their beloved Queen Jemma that was the final straw. Argus used his power of persuasion once again to banish all the boys—except those of Royal blood—from the Realm of the Faeries.

King Ira passed his crown to his son Kendal shortly after mourning his wife, and joined the Ancestral Order. King

Kendal then passed the law that no baby boy born of the Human-Mating Law would be able to remain in the Realm of the Faeries. Only girls were safe. Many generations later, through the research done by the King's Advisors, the Faeries learned how to turn Humans back into Faeries. Goodwin promptly put a stop to it.

"They chose their fate all those years ago. To give them immortal life now would be rewarding their ancestors for fighting beside Fernandez. That would be Treason!"

King Vander did not see it this way and secretly, he had his advisors continue their research. It would be several thousands of years before the Faeries trusted any human enough, not to erase their memory after communicating with them. Her name was Cordellia and she was Queen of the Human race in the town of Wyveren.

# Chapter One:

## A Meeting Of Fate

A young girl of about eight years of age was running happily through the forest. Her red curly hair bounced up and down with every step she took and her reddish brown eyes took in everything they saw. The dark blue gown that she wore danced in the wind that surrounded her and she was not alone.

A pair of sparkling blue eyes peered at her from behind a bush. The eyes watched her laugh and play and then the body to which they belonged moved and snapped a twig. The little girl turned attentively toward the sound.

"Whose there?" She asked.

The pair of eyes tried to stay hidden, but the little girl walked right up to the bush and found them.

"Hello!" She exclaimed.

The eyes stepped away from the bush to reveal a little boy with blonde spiky hair, who was wearing a long serene blue shirt and a pair of long black pants clothed his legs.

Sprouting from the back of his shirt was the most beautiful pair of wings the little girl had ever seen. Her eyes went to them immediately. They were a bright white and lined with silver. She could see each line in every feather. They looked as soft as the clouds looked in the sky.

"Why do you have wings, boy?" She asked with one hand outstretched as though to touch them.

The boy took a step back from the girl. "Don't call me boy! I am a Prince!"

The girl lowered her hand and took another step toward the boy. "Oh! Of what village, are you a Prince in?"

The boy puffed out his chest and took another step toward the girl feeling more comfortable now that he was not in danger of being touched by her. "I am Prince of the Faeries!"

The girl crossed her arms across her chest. "Faeries do not exist!"

The boy had his hands in fists on his hips. "Yes they do! I don't expect you to understand little human girl."

The boy did not intimidate the girl and she advanced on him pointing to herself. "Don't call me girl! I am a Princess!"

The boy continued to tease her, though he took a few steps backwards at her sudden advance. "Yes, a little human Princess!"

"So what, you are a little Faerie Prince!" The girl pointed at him and then promptly stuck her tongue out.

"Oh you think so?! Well I can do this!"

The boy grabbed a rock that was nearby, a rock that both of the children could have sat on comfortably, and lifted it over his head. He then placed it back down and dusted himself off with a smirk at the girl. The girl was very excited about that however and did not invoke the reaction the boy was looking for.

"That is amazing! I want to be a Faerie! Would I be able to do that if I were a Faerie?"

The boy, who was expecting to gloat, sat down on the rock he had just lifted above his head and extended a hand to help her up on the rock. She accepted.

"Well each Faerie is different, so different Faeries have different magic."

"Like what?" The girl questioned.

"Well there is strength, speed, camouflage, memory keepers, time changers, dream walkers, healers, and all other kinds."

The girl was quiet now. She looked at the boy.

"Can you make me a Faerie?"

"I can, but it takes a long time."

"How long?!"

"Well first you have to be older. Once you are a human-made Faerie you stay the age you are when you are turned."

"How old are you?"

"I am four, but I was born a Faerie. We grow up twice as fast as humans until ten and one half years and then we don't age anymore."

The girl made a face at this comment.

"So I am older than you?"

The boy rolled his eyes.

"You have lived some years longer than me yes, but I am your age in appearance; and in a few years I will appear older than you."

The girl seemed to accept this definition.

"What else?"

"Then you have to earn your wings."

"How do I do that?"

"By being good, I am really glad I don't have to earn mine. I was born with them."

"Then what has to happen?"

"You need the love of a Faerie. One who will share themselves with you, and give you some of their magic."

"Oh."

The girl looked intently at the boy before she continued.

"Is there anything else?"

"Yes, once you have all of the other things, your magic will develop. That is when you become a true Faerie. Then you are immortal and will live forever."

The girl became very quiet at this moment. The boy looked at her.

"What is the matter?"

"I wish my mother was a Faerie. She died when I was four. She was sick."

The boy looked sad for the girl.

"I am sorry to hear that."

The girl perked up.

"Thank You, it was a long time ago, and I do not remember much from that day. Would you like to play?"

The boy slid off the rock and then helped the girl down.

"Yes, lets sword fight!"

The girl looked at the ground and crossed her arms. She then meagerly replied.

"I do not know how."

The boy pulled two wooden swords from his little holster.

"Then I shall teach you."

The children played well into the day; sword fighting, hide and seek and they even went for a swim in a nearby river. As the sun was setting, they both knew they needed to go home. The boy was retrieving his wooden swords.

"Hey, Princess, what is your name?"

"My name is Mabli, Princess Mabli of Wyveren, and your name?"

"My name is Dameon, Prince Dameon of the Faeries."

They both smiled at each other as they turned to go their separate ways both knowing they would both be in the same spot the following day.

Six Years Later…

# Chapter Two:

# A Bloodline In Danger

A man was pacing back and forth down a corridor. His red coat flipped up and down with every sharp turn. The man was a round sort of shape and his face held a most anxious expression. A door suddenly opened and another man came out of it. This man wore plain ordinary clothing. He shook his head in the direction of the red coat standing expectantly in the corridor.

"I am sorry King Xavier; this girl is not with child either."

The King gave a scowl and turned to walk away down the corridor. The ordinary looking man walked after him.

"Sire, do not be upset by this. You have a beautiful daughter and you are fortunate enough to have found a Prince who is not in line for his own throne. Therefore, your daughter may rule this Palace. Your bloodline will remain here through her."

The King stopped and turned to be face to face with this ordinary man.

"Doctor, how many girls have you examined for me?"

The doctor paused to think.

"I would imagine it has been at least a dozen in the past six moons My Lord."

The King nodded to himself.

"Not a single one of them has become with child."

The doctor proceeded to answer with caution.

"No Your Highness, not a single one."

The King continued to walk. The doctor followed, listening to him talk to himself.

"How is it possible that not a single girl has become in the family way?"

The doctor piped up before thinking.

"Your Majesty many males become unable to produce offspring at a certain age. Just as the woman ceases to bleed, the male ceases to create. It is a natural part of growing older Sire."

The King now stopped and turned to glare at the doctor.

"You think I have been trying to conceive another child?!"

The doctor nodded slowly but now unsurely.

"Haven't you My Lord? Haven't you been trying to create a male heir?"

The King started to laugh. The doctor started to chuckle at his ease. King Xavier placed his arm around the doctor and continued to walk down the corridor. The doctor was not chuckling anymore.

"No doctor. Those girls I have been having you examine have been with Prince Edward of Stocking."

The doctor's face became pale.

"Princess Mabli's betrothed?"

"Yes. Now tell me doctor, how is it possible that an eighteen-year-old boy in his prime has not yet created at least one life in the past six moons? He has had ample opportunity."

The doctor started to stutter now.

"It...it could...could have been...an illness the boy's mother had while she was with child."

The King stopped their walking and held the doctor at arms length by his shoulders.

"Can it be fixed?"

The doctor's mouth was wide open; he was staring right into the King's eyes.

"I have never heard of such a problem being fixed before."

The King scowled to himself and continued to walk without the doctor.

"I shall have to take care of this problem myself. I should send girls to Prince Henry of Stocking; he is sixteen and should do just as well as Edward. Mabli won't care; she will marry whomever I tell her to!"

# Chapter Three:

## A War Is Started

Mabli came to the rock that she and Dameon usually played at. She was fourteen now and her red hair had straightened and grown long throughout the years. If she were to stand naked, her hair would not only cover her blossoming new breast, but it would also fall beneath her buttocks. Today she came running up to the rock in a buttercup yellow dress that was very becoming on her. When she reached the spot that they had first met, she found a sword sticking straight out of the ground. She plucked it from the earth questioningly and the moment that she did Dameon came running from his hiding place to launch a surprise attack. Mabli was startled at this though she countered him as though she knew all along that this was coming. There was something different about him though she couldn't quite put her finger on what it was. Dameon fought so quickly the breeze made his hair dance. His hair had managed to grow to about shoulder length, still brilliantly blonde. Most days he wore his hair tied at the back of his head this was something Mabli vastly approved of. Her blade grazed across his pale green shirt, but not enough to slice it. Dameon was pleasantly surprised at her speed and gracefulness. He charged at her and she spun out of the way and hit the sword against his back as he past. That was it! His wings were missing. The two faced each other, Dameon with a mischievous smile on his lips and Mabli with a look of shock on her face, but she was not going to let that distract her. They charged at each other and their swords collided into one another. The clanking sound could be heard from miles around. Mabli twirled her weapon around Dameon's and managed to pluck it from his hands. Both children watched the sword flip in the air and both saw it fall feet away from Dameon. He went to reach for it, but Mabli held her blade at his throat. He laughed.

"Okay, okay, you win."

Mabli lowered her weapon and began to laugh with him. She handed him back his sword and they went to sit on their rock. Mabli immediately began to question him.

"What happened to your wings?"

Dameon tilted his head to one side for a moment and suddenly his wings were there. Mabli's eyebrows shot up in surprise.

"How are you doing that Dameon?"

He smiled at her.

"I became of age last night. When a Faerie becomes of age they are able to make their wings disappear, a sort of *right of passage* I assume. You know though, I never realized how in the way they are until I can make them disappear."

Dameon smiled to himself and turned the conversation a different route.

"You have improved so much Mabli. Remind me to never

get into a real battle with you, unless you are on my side that is."

Mabli jumped up suddenly, she remembered why she had run here this morning.

"Dameon, Stocking has declared war against Wyveren!"

Dameon jumped up as Mabli had.

"Why would your neighboring village do that?"

Mabli turned away from Dameon but he ran around to face her.

"What has happened Mabli?"

Mabli looked down at her hands instead of into his eyes.

"Prince Edward was killed on our land yesterday."

Dameon sat back on the rock.

"Prince Edward, is that the middle boy from King Demetrius?"

Mabli turned slowly to face Dameon.

"Yes."

Dameon seemed confused.

"Well, how was he killed?"

Mabli sat back on the rock.

"He went hunting with my Father and took an arrow in the back. Of course it was an accident, but Stocking will hear none of it."

Dameon was silent for a moment and then very slowly phrased his next question.

"Are you sure that it was an accident?"

Mabli drew back her hand to slap Dameon, but took it no further. She slid off the rock and started to walk away. Dameon followed her.

"Mabli, I only meant..."

Mabli cut him off.

"It would make no sense for my father to kill him! He was to be my..."

Mabli threw her hands over her mouth, but Dameon had already guessed.

"You and he were...betrothed?"

Mabli slowly shook her head yes.

"I only found out Dameon. Right before the hunting trip and I was so upset...I have been worrying about this the whole time."

Dameon was confused again.

"Worrying about what?"

Mabli blinked and one tear rolled down her cheek.

"What if I killed him?"

Dameon grabbed Mabli in an embrace and stroked her hair.

"How would you have killed him Mabli?"

Mabli spoke through her sobs.

"What if my magic as a faerie is to wish for things and they actually happen?"

Dameon laughed to himself. Then he pulled Mabli at arms length away and wiped the tears from her face.

"You wished for him to be killed by an arrow in the back?"

Mabli sniffed.

"No, but I wished I did not have to marry him."

Dameon smiled and hugged Mabli tighter.

"You could not be developing your magic yet, because we have not done the ceremony yet."

Mabli pushed herself away from Dameon.

"What ceremony?"

Dameon started to walk and Mabli followed him.

"We must perform a ceremony in front of all the Faeries

for your wings to grow. Otherwise anybody who has been extremely good can sprout them."

Mabli's eyes grew three times their size.

"When can that be done Dameon?"

Dameon laughed.

"Not until we are older Mabli. You don't want to be fourteen years old for the rest of all time do you?"

Mabli shook her head with a frown.

"The thing is Dameon, with the war going on now I am not sure how often I will be able to get out of the castle."

Dameon pulled something out of his shirt and over his head. It was a beautiful pendent it was mainly a sea-green turquoise color along with purple and pink lines going throughout the small piece. It had a dark brown border and was held up on a black string. Mabli could not help being transfixed on it. Dameon placed the necklace around her neck and slipped it under her dress.

"If you wear this Mabli, it will protect you."

Mabli fingered where the pendent lay on her skin.

"Dameon I can't take your pendent."

He held up his hand to silence her.

"It is your pendent. I was going to wait until the ceremony to give it to you, but you need it now."

Mabli stared into Dameon's eyes.

"This is your family pendent."

Dameon kissed her square on the lips. This was the first time he had attempted such a thing on anybody besides his mother and sisters; though he had dreamt of trying it out on Mabli. He pulled away from the kiss and looked Mabli right in her eyes.

"I love you Mabli, and you will be family one day. The pendent will protect you."

Mabli was silent. She was touching her lips and turning a very red color. Dameon felt awful, he had not meant to embarrass her. This was not how he imagined this moment would be. He turned to hide his coloring face when Mabli grabbed his arm, spun him around, and pulled him close to her.

"I love you too Dameon, I always have."

Mabli kissed Dameon as he had kissed her and when they finished both had to take a moment to wipe the wetness away from their lips. Mabli glanced at the sun and noticed it was starting to set.

"I must get back. I don't know when I will see you again."

Dameon embraced her and she rested her head upon his shoulder.

"We will find a way Mabli. We will find a way."

# Chapter Four:

# The Quest

Sluggish footsteps were pulsing down a red carpet leading to a throne. The armor, worn by Zindel, was causing his steps to be like a coming thunderstorm. He approached the end of the carpet, removed his battle beaten helmet, and knelt at the throne. As he did, so dust and dried blood flew into the air. His blonde hair fell into his blue eyes as he glanced at the king. His pink lips were slightly chapped and formed his words.

"King Xavier, you have sent for me?"

The King disposed of a chicken bone he was gnawing on, tossing it on to the golden platter at his right. He then wiped his greasy hands and pudgy face with a golden linen napkin. The king had grown quite rotund over the past five years. The doctor explained it as stress from the on-going war, so much so, that his overcoat was bulging at the ruby red buttons. He had just acquired this coat not a fortnight ago and was already in dire need of another. The King reminded Zindel of a gargantuan pig. Upon his head was a crown of gold. His red hair was sticking out of it and was plastered to his skin from his perspiration, for it was the middle of the summer season and for this particular meeting he had dismissed his fanning servants.

"Yes Zindel, I have."

He paused to cough, and drank a bit of wine out of his golden goblet. Zindel cringed as he watched the wine dribble down the many chins on his neck.

"I'm sure you have heard by now that Princess Mabli has been ill for some time. She has, I'm afraid, taken a turn for the worst."

He said this with bits of food spewing from his mouth. He paused, waiting for a reaction. Zindel stood motionless. The King continued smacking his greasy lips, for he saw another plate of food coming. Zindel finally spoke.

"What can I do My Lord? Shall I journey to the next town for their best doctor?"

The King wearily took his gaze away from his plate, which was just now arriving at the table in front of him.

"No, no. It is not a doctor she needs. What Mabli needs Zindel is The Golden Staff of Enchantment. Have you heard of it?"

"No My Lord, I have not."

The King chuckled at this.

"It does not surprise me lad. There are few who have. As it is, the Golden Staff was a gift to Princess Mabli from her mother. The last gift she ever received from her. Mabli was out in the woods a few weeks ago and she took it with her. It was stolen from her by the hands of a," he paused as if what he was about to say was a horrible taste in his mouth, "a... faerie."

Zindel's eyes widened. He had heard rumors of the King's obsession with Faeries, he had heard more so of Princess Mabli's, but he did not believe the King entertained the idea much past stories.

"Sir King, what good could a golden staff do for Princess Mabli?"

"What good could it do, Zindel?!?"

The King exclaimed shifting his elephantine gut from side to side attempting to stand on his short portly legs. After a moment, he began to breathe heavily and his face turned a violent shade of purple. His tantrum subsided and he picked up the grapes on his plate and started to pop one into his mouth at a time while he continued to carry on his conversation.

"It was not until a week or so after the Golden Staff was stolen that I started to realize that she was looking paler than I had ever seen her look before. The Golden Staff holds magical powers, healing powers. That is why she has never been sick before."

Zindel was still confused.

"My Lord, what could a faerie want with Princess Mabli's golden staff? They have magical powers of their own, do they not?"

"Yes my dear boy, they do. However, the Dark Faeries need human magic. You see, all anybody needs to take over a species is the magic they hold; I can only hope that the faerie that did steal the Golden Staff was attracted to it because it was made of gold and not because it holds human magic."

Zindel knew that the King spoke to truth.

"Zindel, I need you to enter the Realm of the Faeries and retrieve the Golden Staff of Enchantment. Though you must not go alone! The world of the Faeries is a dangerous one.

They lure many innocent knights, like you, into their world forever."

Zindel looked taken aback slightly. Never in his wildest dreams would he have expected his King to ask him this.

"I can't My Lord."

The King erupted in anger. He threw his plate across the room. Then he calmly snapped his fingers and a third plate came out of a side room and was placed in the exact location of the others. This seemed to settle the King. He grabbed a loaf of bread and spoke as calm as could be to Zindel.

"Why do you feel that you can not take this mission?"

"My Lord, we are in the middle of a war with Stocking! I alone am leading many men out there. How can you expect me to just up and leave them?"

"Zindel you are the best knight I have. There is no question in my mind that you are the best knight for this quest. You will leave those men because it is what your King commands! However I cannot spare any other Knights to accompany you. You must recruit men from the village."

Zindel looked into the King's eyes.

"Good King, you want me to bring a bunch of inexperienced men on an extremely dangerous quest? How can I stake my life on them when I know they do not have what it takes?"

The King gave a loud sigh that signaled he was done discussing things with Zindel.

"You may train them before you leave. I shall give you five days for this."

Zindel had to hold in his laughter.

"Train farmers and blacksmiths in five days! You must think I am a miracle worker good King! I need at least ten days time."

"Seven. That is my final offer Zindel."

Zindel nodded defiantly and then attempted to plead once more with the King.

"This quest, My Lord, I guarantee that none of the men I take with me will come back. It seems an unnecessary risk for the people of your kingdom. If the Faeries sense trespass, they will put aside the peace that has been between our two worlds."

The King now kept his temper, but was beginning to turn purple in the face.

"Zindel, they violated the peace when they stole from my daughter. Now to not help the Princess of your kingdom is an unspeakable crime, but more so, if you do not come back with the Golden Staff of Enchantment, I shall have your head."

Zindel angrily bowed once more, replaced his helmet, and left the King who was now starting to gnaw on a pork chop. Zindel set off to the village to gather a group of men to venture with him. He stood in the town square, and assembled a town meeting.

# Chapter Five:

## Village Men

"People of Wyveren, I am Zindel, a knight for the King. King Xavier has informed me that Princess Mabli has taken a turn for the worse. Her only hope of recovery is for a group of valiant men to venture deep into the Realm of the Faeries and retrieve her Golden Staff of Enchantment. All who wish to accompany me on this quest step forward and say 'Aye'."

The town was quiet. Nobody seemed to move or even breathe. Zindel's pride was slowly vanishing too. The Realm of Faeries he must have sounded like the town loon. He was just thinking of turning around and starting the venture on his own when one single, solitary hand shot up in the air.

"Aye!"

A small voice cried out. The grubby brown hand belonged to a boy of sixteen. He had curly blonde hair with green eyes. He wore a green vest and a green hat. His pants were brown and his shoes were made of wood. He worked his way through the crowd, until he stood beside Zindel. Zindel eyed the boy queerly.

"You're name, Son?"

"Bevyn is my name, Sir Zindel. I humbly wish to accompany you on your quest because," he paused as if thinking of a valid reason, "Well, no one else seems to want to."

Zindel laughed meagerly at this comment.

"We have one addition to this quest; however, many more are needed. Remember men your Princess needs you."

The boy's courage encouraged others. Hands began to rise, the bodies to which they belonged stepped forward, and the meeting went on. The second man to step up to Zindel was a stout man with straight, brown hair and blue eyes. He was pudgy around the face, and he looked as though he had some years on Zindel. He shyly stood in front of Zindel.

"Hello, I'm Razial."

The third to venture through the crowd was towering and scrawny. His arms looked like the very chicken bones the king had been eating earlier that day. His hair was a reddish brown color, as were his eyes. His parents accompanied him, though they did not implore him to stay. It was as if he was non-existent to them, and it showed through his eyes.

"I'm Tristram."

He said, waving a scrawny arm above his head. The next man was very beauteous. His hair was a rippling golden blonde, and his eyes were gorgeously blue. His muscles could be seen through his vest, and he was indeed the want of every woman in the land. He approached Zindel running one hand through his hair.

"Hello, I'm Gwynn."

Even his name rolled off his tongue handsomely. The

next boy however was much different. He stood crooked, his gloomy eyes looked untrustworthy. He had a wicked blackness under both of them, which could have been years of soot caked on. When he talked, you could sense the evil tone in his voice. His hair looked greasy and dirty, he smelled putrid, and he looked dishonest and impure.

"I'm Braen."

He said sticking his hand out. Zindel hesitated before shaking it. The next man looked like snow. His hair was luminously blonde, and his grey eyes were so incandescent they were almost white. He wore beige clothing, which was about the only thing that toned him down.

"I'm Erwin, and glad to be on your team!"

Zindel laughed a nice hearty laugh.

"Yes, you can light the way at night."

"And I can light the fires! I'm Kay."

Who, on the other hand, was a fiery red. He had red hair and eyes that were almost orange. His freckles accounted for the tan in his face, but the rest of him was a fine red, like sunburn. The next man bumped into Zindel's waist. Zindel looked down and the man waved to him.

"Hi, I'm Cole."

He was dwarfed, with brown wavy hair, and green eyes.

"And I am Dagon!"

Dagon was also interesting. He was the equal of Cole in looks. They could have been twins, but they were not acting very brotherly. Maybe they were distant cousins.

"Move over! Leave room for me! Hey there Zindel, I'm Kyle."

Kyle was another diminutive man acquired to the group. He had a shaved head and green eyes. He had a bronze like color on his skin. Then someone opposite came walking up.

"Come now Kyle, push over and let a real man join! I'm Owen, where do I sign?"

Owen was tall and muscular as well. He had straight dark brown hair, and eyes so blue that they sparkled next to sapphires.

"Is there any room left? I'm Awstin."

Awstin was one of the only men to have wavy brown hair and brown eyes to match. He was a tall and muscular addition. All of a sudden, Dagon squealed with delight.

"I knew you couldn't stay away Morgan!"

Morgan was the best friend of Dagon. He had curly red hair and he was on the pudgy side.

"I snuck away from my parents, but I don't think they noticed, I'm Seith."

Seith was a tall man, he was somewhat muscular. He had wavy brown hair, and blue eyes. Finally, the last man to approach Zindel was Kyle's brother. He was tall and scrawny; he also had a shaved head and green eyes. Also like his brother, he had a bronze color in his skin.

"Hello Zindel, I'm Trent."

After meeting briefly with each of these men, Zindel led them back to the castle grounds. Where they spent the remainder of the day setting up their sleeping quarters, learning how to start fires and how to keep them burning. Zindel sighed as he sat by his fire that night and thought of the next seven days. He looked out at the courtyard and saw several burning fires in front of several sleeping men.

"They will never be ready for this. I should be fighting the war instead of training blacksmiths and chimney sweeps for a quest."

Zindel rolled over and went to sleep.

# Chapter Six:

## Swords

Zindel woke the men just as the first bit of the sun could be seen. Once they had all sleepily gathered around him he started to talk about his sword.

"This piece of metal has saved my life more times than I can...yes Bevyn?"

The boy was practically jumping up and down.

"Excuse me Sir Zindel, but can we start after breakfast?"

Zindel's face fell.

"Start after breakfast?"

Zindel noticed that all the men were nodding their heads in agreement. He gave a long sigh.

"You have until the sun has risen."

The men dispersed quickly for it was half way showing already. Zindel went back to his sleeping area, sat by his glowing embers, and angrily started talking to himself.

"Start after breakfast. Ha! If they wanted to eat they

should have eaten before the sun started to show first light, instead of sleeping in."

Zindel called the men back to his attention and many came back with food in their hands to finish eating as Zindel started his lesson.

"As I was saying," Zindel picked up his sword, "this piece of metal has saved my life more time than I can count. It will be of great value to you on this Quest. We will start by having everyone pick out his own sword. King Xavier has graciously allotted one for every man."

The moment that Zindel pointed the direction to the arsenal Owen showed no hesitation. He led the group of men to it, picked up one of the swords, and with one hand held it out at arms length. Then he placed the weapon on two of his fingers where the handle ended and the blade began to check for balance. After that, he swung the sword with both arms over his head down toward the earth. He proceeded to swing the sword from side to side. Owen tried this with many different swords before choosing one to his liking. Zindel was pleasantly surprised. He walked over to Owen.

"Where did you learn to choose your weapon in such a fashion?"

Owen smiled at him.

"Zindel, I come from a family of sword smiths. My family probably made most of these swords. So when you make the swords you know how to check for flaws."

Many of the other men began to pick out their swords in this manner. Zindel thought to himself that perhaps not all was lost.

Once the men had picked out their weapons, Zindel stood in front of them all and tried to teach them the basics of sword fighting. Bevyn picked up on the basics quickly

Zindel thought, though showed very little talent on the more advanced movements. Zindel walked over to him.

"I thought perhaps you were a quick leaner little lad, yet you seem to be having trouble."

Bevyn smiled at Zindel and let his sword fall as he turned to address him.

"I am afraid I am not a fast learner, even though I am a squire. My mentor and I had started going over the basics of sword fighting, but then the war started. I have practiced the basics everyday these past five years, but I have no one to teach me further."

Zindel almost had to laugh at this.

"Well my dear boy, diligence, and persistence are key components to becoming a good knight. I see that you have mastered both. Tell me Bevyn, who is the knight you squire for?"

Bevyn picked up his sword again and went back to trying the advance movements.

"Sir Arthur."

Zindel faltered for a moment.

"Bevyn, I am surprised the word has not yet reached you. Sir Arthur was killed in battle just a fortnight ago."

Bevyn's sword fell again.

"How can I become a knight now?"

Zindel smiled at the boy.

"Cheer up little lad. You can find a new knight to squire for."

Bevyn did not cheer up.

"Nobody will want a sixteen year old who has only mastered basics. Besides that every Knight available is fighting the war."

Zindel frowned wishing he could still be one of them.

"Not every Knight."

Bevyn became truly excited all at once.

"That is right! Sir Zindel, you are not fighting the war! This might be presumptuous of me, but Sir Zindel, might I become your squire?"

Zindel had never received such an offer before. Nobody wanted to be squire to him, even though he was one of the elite Knights in King Xavier's court. He always assumed it was because he had come from another town fifteen years ago. Nobody knew his background. Zindel stared at the village boy who desperately wanted guidance and a mentor.

"You may become my squire, Bevyn."

Zindel was not quite sure why he had agreed to such an arrangement, but he knew he was happy that he had.

After stopping for a mid-day meal, Zindel paired the men up, himself with Bevyn, and started to teach them in the ways of combat. Owen outshined everybody. The men fought until there was hardly any daylight left. Zindel dismissed them to dinner and then to sleep. He watched all the men as they tried to start their fires without his instruction tonight. Kay was the fastest to start his fire. Then Zindel watched as Kay went around and started to help other's start theirs. After dinner, Zindel walked over to Kay's sleeping quarters and sat down next to him.

"How do you expect the men to learn how to start their own fires if you do it for them?"

Kay laughed at this question.

"I did not start their fires for them Zindel, I simply helped them to remember how to do it. Besides, when we are out on our quest we are only going to have one fire a night, correct?"

Zindel hesitantly nodded and Kay continued.

"Not all of us are going to be doing everything."

Zindel looked at Kay.

"What do you mean?"

Kay pointed toward Razial.

"He is a great hunter. I am sure you will see that for yourself before we venture out on this quest. However because he is a great hunter, I doubt that you will have him searching for water when we stop at night. Unless you want every one to get their own dinner, find their own water, and build their own fires, then not everybody will be doing everything."

Zindel leaned closer as though he was going to whisper to Kay.

"That is true, however let us just assume that you get taken or killed on this quest. Who then will know how to start the fires?"

Kay was silenced. Zindel stood up and went back to his own fire.

# Chapter Seven:

## A Visit To Mabli's Window

Mabli had been at her bedroom window all day watching the men learn how to sword fight. She laughed, as some of them could not grasp the simplest concepts of battle. She did not know why her father was gathering more fighters, perhaps the war had taken a turn for the worse, and they needed new men. As Mabli looked at herself in the mirror, she noticed how pale she looked. She had not eaten all day and yet she felt no pains of hunger. She took a tool used for untangling ones hair and stroked it through her own. She heard the sound of a plunk on her window, as though something had hit it. She was still for a moment and the sound came again. Mabli placed the hair tool down and walked over to her window. As she pulled back the curtains, she saw Dameon starring back at her through the glass. She gave a mini squeal of delight and opened the window for him to crawl into her room from the tree branch he was presently perched upon. He bounded in and no sooner had Mabli closed the window again had Dameon wrapped her up in his arms. She returned the embrace deeply and for a long moment, they just sat holding each other. Mabli spoke with happiness flooding her voice.

"Oh Dameon I am so happy to see you! It has been more than a fortnight though, what has kept you?"

Dameon smiled at Mabli, even though her tone had turned to accusatory, he still loved to hear her voice.

"I have had business to attend to in the Realm of the Faeries. I have been in with the council for three weeks straight my love, but I bring good news!"

Mabli could hardly contain her excitement.

"Well you must tell me at once!"

Dameon sat her down on her bed and then knelt before her.

"I have gotten permission for the ceremony to be performed."

Mabli cried with delight before she could stop herself. Then she calmed down and began to look perplexed.

"Dameon, I am only nineteen years old. Isn't it still too soon for me?"

Dameon sat beside her on the bed.

"Technically yes, but that is why I was before the council for so long. I have convinced them that we cannot wait for the years to pass because you are in danger with the war."

Mabli smiled again.

"So they approved! Oh Dameon you have no idea how happy I am."

Dameon smiled at her.

"You cannot possibly be half as happy as I am my dear Princess."

Mabli walked around the room now.

"When will it happen? Do we have to go tonight?"

Dameon laughed at his pacing love.

"No my dear, we do not have to go tonight. More planning and preparations must be made before they will be ready."

Dameon now took on a more serious face and Mabli gave him an equally serious one.

"What is it Dameon?"

He took her hand in his.

"Once we do this ceremony Mabli, there is no going back."

Mabli began to smile at Dameon.

"What a silly boy you are. I would never dream of turning back."

Dameon shook his head.

"It is not just about becoming a faerie Mabli. Once this ceremony is performed, as far as everyone is concerned we are betrothed for marriage."

Mabli kept smiling at him.

"I thought as much, but Dameon if this is your idea of a proposal I shall have you know that most suitors bring a gift of some kind."

Dameon then produced a small box from his pocket. Mabli was rendered speechless. Dameon opened it and produced a thin silver chain. He took the pendent from around Mabli's neck and transferred it from the black string to the silver chain. He then presented it to her. Mabli picked it up delicately between her fingers.

"Oh Dameon it is so beautiful. I have never seen metal like this before."

Dameon smiled at her.

"It is from the Realm of the Faeries. This metal is some of the strongest in the world."

Mabli went to place it around her neck when Dameon took it from her.

"Allow me."

He stood behind her and they both faced the mirror, he lifted the necklace over her head and let the pendent fall beneath her dress. He kissed her on the cheek once the necklace was securely on. Mabli turned around quickly and kissed him on the lips. Dameon's ears perked up suddenly.

"Somebody is coming."

Dameon jumped into her closet as the door to her bedroom opened. A guard stepped into the room.

"Is everything alright Princess? I thought I heard voices?"

Mabli smiled sweetly at the guard and assured him that he was imaging the voices he heard for it was only herself in the room. The guard glanced around once more and then closed the door. Dameon came out from hiding. They both had to speak in whispers now.

"The security is much higher than usual. Sneaking in here tonight was more of a challenge, what with the Knights in the courtyard."

Mabli took a seat by her window to watch them again.

"They are not knights, most are village men. They came last night. I think they are being trained for the war. Stocking must be advancing."

Dameon gave a grave expression.

"I must have them hurry the preparations for the ceremony. I will come to get you Mabli when it is time."

Mabli stood and embraced Dameon again. They shared a passionate kiss before he left her.

"It should not be more than a few days time and then I will return to you."

Mabli kissed him once more and she watched him climb down the tree before shutting her window.

# Chapter Eight:

## Bows and Arrows

By the time Zindel awoke the next morning Bevyn was at his side. Zindel started with surprise. Bevyn chuckled.

"Sorry to wake you Sir Zindel. I was just trying to get your fire going again so we could start cooking breakfast."

Zindel glanced around him. Nobody else had woken and there was no sign of the first morning light yet.

"Bevyn, why are you not at your own quarters resting?"

Bevyn was poking hopeless at the fire with a stick.

"I have rested Sir Zindel and the sun is about to rise; besides a good squire is always awake before his knight to assist him with the morning chores."

Zindel took the stick from the boy, for he had actually put more of the embers out, and gave the fire a few well-chosen pokes before he blew onto it with his breath. The fire flared up into several flames licking the air around them. Zindel sent Bevyn to get their morning rations and when he returned the sky was turning a very dark pink, the sun was rising.

By the time there was enough daylight to see, both Zindel and Bevyn had finished their breakfast and Zindel rudely awoke the rest of the men. They sleepily gathered around. Zindel started his speech but was interrupted by an audaciously loud yawn. Zindel searched the crowd and found the face it belonged to. He was twirling his fine golden hair in his strong muscular fingers and he yawned again, obnoxiously loud. Zindel cleared his throat. Gwynn showed no response. Zindel finally spoke.

"Gwynn, am I boring you?"

Gwynn looked up surprised.

"No, not at all, but I am waiting for you to dismiss us for breakfast. You will go over all this again once we have eaten."

Zindel had been too soft on them the previous morning. By giving into Bevyn's request Zindel had shown the men that they could expect this kind of break every morning. Zindel spoke loudly to the entire group.

"This will be the last morning I give any of you time to eat. From now on, we start each lesson at sunrise. If you have not eaten by then, you must hold off until the next meal. You have ten minutes to eat this morning and if any of you come back with breakfast, you will be polishing everybody else's sword tonight, dismissed."

The men scurried. In ten minutes time the men were back in place and only one person disobeyed Zindel and brought his breakfast with him.

"Gwynn, you will see me tonight after lessons."

Gwynn quickly finished his meal but did not seem

perturbed by Zindel's punishment. Zindel led the men out to the King's courtyard where three targets had been set up.

"Form a line behind each bow, five to a line please."

Bevyn, the pudgy, brown hair and blue eyed one—Zindel thought his name was Razial and the tall scrawny one— Tristram, were the first to step up to the bows. Zindel gave more commands.

"Load the arrows."

Bevyn picked up an arrow and eyed it suspiciously. It was easy enough to tell the boy had never even seen a bow and arrow, let alone shot one. Zindel sighed and went to show Bevyn how it was loaded. The pudgy one had no trouble. Zindel noticed that he was a quick loader and he had his arrow and bow pointed at the ground awaiting the next instruction. The scrawny one seemed to know what he was doing, but he was extremely slow. Zindel called the next set of orders.

"Ready the bows," Pudgy held his bow arms length away with the arrow pointed at the target the other two followed his example. "Aim," He pulled the arrow and string back to his chin and held it there. Scrawny followed, Bevyn could not pull the string all the way back to his chin. "Release," Razial let go of his string and his arrow sailed perfectly into the middle circle on his target. Bevyn let go and his arrow fell short of the target. Tristram let go and it flew to the right side of the target. Zindel was impressed with Razial.

"Retrieve your arrows."

The next three to step up were Gwynn, the one who looked dirty and gave Zindel a sense of disease—Braen Zindel suddenly recalled and Erwin—the one who was fair skinned. Gwynn's arrow soared right over the target. The dark one's arrow struck the target in one of the outer circles and the luminescent one's arrow grazed the left side of the target but did not stick. Kay, the one who knew how to pick his swords—Owen was his name--and the man with wavy brown hair and brown eyes—Zindel believed his name was Awstin--were next. Kay's arrow hit one of the outer circles, as did Owen's. Clearly, he was a better swords man than an archer. Awstin hit one of the inner circles. The dwarfs—Cole, Dagon and Morgan were next. All three of their arrows flew under the targets. The tall man with wavy brown hair and blue eyes—Seith, Zindel recalled, and two men who resembled each other, probably brothers Zindel assumed—Trent and Kyle were last to shoot. Seith's arrow skimmed the left side of the target but did not stick. Both Trent and Kyle's arrows soared right into the center ring of their own targets. Zindel silently rejoiced. He had at least three experienced archers among his group. He circled the men through this exercise until all of them, with the exception of Bevyn, had at least hit the target somewhere. He dismissed them for their mid-day break. Bevyn came up to Zindel very solemnly.

"Zindel," Zindel nodded to acknowledge the boy. "Do you regret taking me on as a squire?"

Zindel was shocked at this question. He looked at Bevyn and could see that the boy was trying very hard to hold himself together. A softer tone came to Zindel's voice.

"I do not Bevyn. I know your training came to a halt and you are only as advanced as a novice."

Bevyn started to come undone.

"It does not bother you that my arrow cannot even fly to the target?"

Zindel beckoned the boy to sit next to him.

"Bevyn, your arrow does not fly to the target because you do not have the strength to pull the string back farther. Your aim was fine I saw the arrow before it fell. The arrow was heading right for the center ring of the target."

Bevyn wiped his tears away as they appeared.

"I do not sword fight well at all."

Zindel nodded in agreement.

"It is true that you are not very talented in these areas, but Bevyn it is not your fault. Your Knight went to war, he could not teach you further."

Bevyn glanced at the fire before him, cooking Zindel's lunch.

"I practically put your fire out this morning."

Zindel turned seriously to Bevyn.

"Do you regret asking to be my squire?"

Bevyn hurriedly shook his head.

"No Sir Zindel. I was just trying to prepare myself for if you were thinking about changing your mind."

Zindel found this odd and cocked his head at the boy.

"Who else changed their mind about you?"

Bevyn looked down at the ground and Zindel persisted in asking.

"Did you have another mentor before Sir Arthur?"

Bevyn nodded and Zindel questioned him further.

"Who was it?"

Bevyn sighed.

"My father, he decided that I showed very little talent as a squire and took on another boy instead. Sir Arthur was a friend of my father's and he always said that I was a huge favor and that my father owed him."

Zindel was taken aback. He never thought a father would choose another over his own son. Zindel smiled at the boy.

"Well Bevyn, you are my squire now and nobody else can have you."

Bevyn smiled up at Zindel and Zindel continued to speak.

"We will just have to work harder at your skills."

After lunch, Zindel had rigged one of the targets on a rope so that it was mobile. One at a time, the men shot at the moving target. Razial, Trent, and Kyle were the only men to hit the center circle every time. After lessons, as promised the men had their orders to drop their swords off at Gwynn's sleeping quarters. Gwynn did not seem to mind however. As soon as a sword was clean, enough to show his reflection he considered it well polished and returned it to its owner. Zindel walked around the camp and talked to his star shooters. They were talking amongst themselves about their techniques.

"So how did you three end up to be such great shots with a bow and arrow?"

The men turned to Zindel. Trent and Kyle responded together.

"Our father taught us."

Zindel smiled.

"That is right, you two are brothers."

Zindel eyed Razial.

"You wouldn't happen to be their father would you?"

Razial chuckled to himself and then stared mournfully into the fire.

"No, I am just a fan of hunting myself."

Zindel pointed toward Kay who was trying to teach Bevyn how to start a fire.

"Razial, do you know that man?"

Razial glanced up.

"Yes, he is a neighbor to my parents. Kay I think his name is. Why do you ask?"

Zindel smiled to himself.

"I just want to know how much everyone knows every body else."

Razial smiled to himself.

"Does he know me then?"

Zindel watched as Bevyn finally got a flame in his fire pit.

"Yes, he knows you are an excellent hunter."

Razial starred in the direction of the newly started fire. Zindel walked back to his own quarters for dinner. Kay and Bevyn were sitting around his fire.

"Sir Zindel look I started this fire!"

Zindel gave a side ways glance at Kay.

"You mean nobody helped you?"

Bevyn was cooking his dinner.

"Well Kay told me what to do, but I did it all myself."

Kay started to defend him self.

"I have found that most people learn better by doing."

Zindel smiled.

"I was not going to chastise. Tell me Kay, how well do you know Razial?"

"I know that he lives with his parents."

Bevyn laughed aloud.

"He is too old to live with his parents!"

Kay smiled at the boy.

"It was not always so. About ten years ago he moved back in with them after his house burned down."

Bevyn's smile was removed immediately from his face. Zindel questioned on.

"How did it start?"

Kay furrowed his eyebrows.

"Nobody really knows that part. All I know is that his

wife and little girl were in that house and neither of them made it out."

# Chapter Nine:

# A Turn For The Worse

A Knight came running up to King Xavier's throne. He collapsed at the King's feet. King Xavier was so startled by this he dropped the leg of the pig he was about to bite into. The Knight was extending his hand toward him. King Xavier grimaced and called upon his servants to help lift the obviously tired Knight to his feet. Xavier waited until after the Knight had a sip of water, before addressing his obvious reason for being there.

"What news do you bring?"

The Knight stood as straight as could be as he answered.

"Stocking has broken through the northern boarder, and their men have made it through."

Xavier's eyes widened at this news. He started to look back and forth as though his eyes were doing the pacing for his body.

"We are awaiting your orders Sire."

Xavier looked grave. Usually Zindel told the men what to

do. That or Zindel would come to the King for permission or approval, but nobody ever asked the King to tell them. The Knight seemed to sense his King's unsure ness.

"Shall I go and ask Sir Zindel?"

Xavier almost shouted here.

"No! Zindel is to know nothing of this. I have set him on a task and if he hears about this incident he will abandon what I have asked him to do and return to the war."

The knight gave the King a confused look.

"Your majesty how could Sir Zindel disobey a direct order?"

King Xavier took offense to this knight's tone.

"Zindel has spent a fair amount of time in punishment for disobeying orders, but his heart is usually in the right place…"

King Xavier looked up and realized he was showing a softer side of himself, a softer side that would place his judgment in danger. He yelled at the knight.

"I SAID ZINDEL IS NOT TO KNOW WHY ARE YOU QUESTIONING ME?!"

The knight nodded his head in understanding.

"Well then Sire, I am awaiting orders."

Xavier tried to think of what Zindel had done in previous situations.

"Retreat further back and create a barrier around the town. It is a smaller territory and will be easier to defend than the whole of Wyveren."

The Knight nodded to his King.

"Do you require anything else My Lord?"

Xavier thought for a moment.

"Yes, we need more protection, especially around Princess Mabli. King Demetrious might be searching for revenge through my daughter. In fact, let no one in or out of her room unless you have my orders to do so."

The Knight again nodded his understanding and took off to fulfill the wishes of his King. Xavier hung his head. He was at a complete loss without Zindel, but what Zindel had to do was equally important and just as vital as the war.

# Chapter Ten:

## Faerie Repellents

On the third morning, Zindel awoke to find Bevyn cooking both of their breakfasts over his fire. As he looked around the camp, he realized that about half of the men were awake also. At sunrise the men were assembled and in their usual place. Gwynn was looking quite sour faced this morning. As Zindel started, he raised his hand.

"Are we really not breaking for breakfast any more?"

Zindel was not amused.

"I thought I made myself clear yesterday. If you have not eaten by the time the lesson starts, you must go without until our mid-day break."

Gwynn responded.

"Well I didn't suppose you meant it."

Zindel had little patience for this.

"Well I did Gwynn, now you know for tomorrow morning."

Gwynn looked taken aback but remained silent through the lesson. Zindel sat the men underneath the shade of the trees in the King's courtyard today. He pulled a bag off his belt and handed similar looking sacks to each man. The men were unsure what they should do with their bags. Zindel saw their unsure ness and as soon as everybody had one, he began his lesson.

"This sack I am giving to each of you is not provided by King Xavier. It is provided by me and it contains faerie repellents."

A hand shot up in the air. Zindel followed the arm down to the face it belonged too. The greasy black hair sat unruly about the dreary hollow of his eyes. Zindel called upon him.

"Yes Braen, you have a question?"

The caked on soot lines under his eyes smiled as he did.

"Why would we need faerie repellents? I thought we needed to talk to them."

Zindel shifted his weight as he considered the best way to answer.

"Yes, we do need to talk to the faeries, but the repellents are for our protection when we are not seeking them."

Braen's hand shot up again. Zindel sighed and nodded his acknowledgement to him.

"We are going on a quest, seeking faeries. I do not see where we will need repellents of any kind."

Zindel cleared his throat. He did not want to scare off any of his men before the quest really started.

"Some of the faeries, resent humans and they will not be helpful to us at all. In fact they will make trouble that is certain to slow us down in our task of locating the Golden Staff of Enchantment."

Braen did not even bother to raise his hand this time.

"So we will encounter evil?"

Zindel considered the group of men in front of him and decided to answer truthfully.

"Yes."

Braen's eyebrows raised in a surprised content. Zindel continued his lesson. He instructed his men to open their bags. Zindel first pulled out a small silver bell. He gave it a little jingle.

"A bell's ring is a repellent to faeries. The bell will work against any evil spirits and it will also cancel out any evil magic cast by a faerie as long as the faerie is present."

Zindel took a seat on a strategically placed rock in front of the men. He placed the bell beside him on the rock. His hand went next to his sword.

"Iron will take a faeries power away for a particular action. For example, if there is any kind of iron in a door, the faerie cannot close it. In your bags, you all will find a long thin piece of iron on a string. Wear it around your neck because it will prevent you from being taken while you sleep."

Zindel placed his own necklace around himself and the others followed his example.

"Fire is also a repellent. Burning embers thrown at any approaching faerie will drive them away. As we cannot carry burning embers in our sacks it is very important for every one to learn how to make a fire."

Zindel said this while looking at Kay. Kay pretended not to notice. Zindel pulled a tasty looking, flat circular, hard patty out of his bag next. Each one had a hole directly in the center of it. Before Zindel could start his explanation on what these were, he heard a very loud crunch. Zindel looked directly at Gwynn, who was chewing on half of his cake.

"Gwynn these are not to be eaten!"

Gwynn swallowed the bit in his mouth.

"Why? Are they poisonous?"

Zindel had crossed his arms across his chest while giving Gwynn a stern look.

"No, they are oatmeal cakes."

Gwynn smiled and stuffed the other half into his mouth.

"I knew they tasted familiar! My mother used to make them for me. They could use a bit of flavor though."

Zindel noticed that at least the rest of the men had the sense to listen to him.

"These oatmeal cakes when carried in one's pocket, prevents a faerie from venturing near you. Gwynn you will have to have yours replaced."

Gwynn was licking his fingers and not paying the least amount of attention to Zindel. Zindel moved next to a medium sized container filled with a white substance. It was in a crystallized form. The men had taken their out and were eyeing it suspiciously.

"This is salt; because we will be in the realm of the faeries, any food we might catch will be considered theirs. Before any food is consumed, it must be sprinkled with salt because the salt will cancel the faeries power of control in the food. It is also likely to overwhelm faeries if tossed at them."

This was the last item in the bag. The men began to repack their repellents. As Zindel watched them he noticed that of the three dwarfed men, only two of them seemed to be conversing with one another. He walked over to those two. One had wavy brown hair and green eyes and was skinny compared to his conversation partner, who had red curly hair and green eyes. Zindel stooped down on one knee to talk to them.

"Are you the other set of brothers?"

They both burst into laughter holding onto their sides and doubling over. Finally, when they could control themselves again Dagon, the brown haired one answered.

"No, Morgan here is my best friend. Cole is my twin."

Zindel detected coldness in Dagon's voice. He would not even grace Cole with the name brother. Zindel decided to sit next to them.

"I am surprised that Cole is not here with you. Most brothers do not leave each other's side."

Morgan now spoke.

"Well Cole always was one of those queer characters."

Zindel furrowed his eyebrows.

"What do you mean?"

Dagon answered him.

"We come from a family of fisherman. Both Cole and I had our sea legs before we could even crawl. However, as Cole grew older he wanted nothing to do with the sea. He wanted to be in the woods, all the time. Well my parents tolerated it to their graves and as soon as they passed Cole moved out, into a tree of all things."

Zindel made a mental note of this before speaking his mind.

"Yet fate has thrown you three together again."

Zindel pointed to the lonely looking dwarf trying to repack his bag as it was when he had received it. Dagon and Morgan looked at Cole before turning back to Zindel.

"Fate has nothing to do with it Sir Zindel," Dagon commented. "Morgan and I came because we have a sense of duty to our Princess. Cole came because we are going to be venturing into the woods."

Zindel did not hesitate to give a response.

"Everybody has a different reason for being here. Fate has stolen the Golden Staff of Enchantment and given us a reason to come together. The mere fact that both you and your brother volunteered is that something greater is trying to send you a message. Do not ignore it Dagon."

Zindel walked away and left the two dwarfed men sitting silently to themselves. After the mid-day meal, Zindel set the men practicing with either the bow and arrows or the swords. Zindel worked with Bevyn on both and noticed a vast improvement in the boy's footing. Handling the sword was something he still had to master. Bevyn was able to pull the arrow back far enough to hit the target, but it bounced right off. Zindel was right about Bevyn's aim though, it bounced off the center ring.

That night around the fire, Zindel noticed that Morgan and Dagon had not invited Cole to join them as he hoped they would. He excused himself from Kay and Bevyn and went to sit with the lonely looking dwarf.

"Hello Cole."

Cole started slightly before looking up at Zindel.

"Oh, hello there Sir Zindel, I was not expecting you."

Zindel sat next to him.

"I talked with Dagon and Morgan earlier today."

Cole smiled at him.

"Dagon told you how I was the strange child?"

Zindel starred into the fire.

"He mentioned that you were twins."

Cole looked at him.

"Usually he denies any relation."

Zindel smiled.

"Well you two look so similar I think it would be impossible to deny in a group this small."

Cole glanced over at his brother and Morgan.

"Yet he has found a way to ignore me completely."

Zindel leaned forward now.

"I cannot believe that this rift between you is simply because you preferred the land to the sea."

Cole chuckled to himself.

"No, but the real rift is because I was a land lover."

Zindel leaned back onto his elbows.

"I do not understand."

Cole also leaned back.

"Dagon and Morgan and I were all very close, even though I would not go fishing with them. When Dagon turned eighteen, he fell in love with the neighbor girl. Her name was Lucy and he courted her for a while. Our father had given him is own boat and he and Morgan had plans to start their own fishing company. Now that he had a way to support Lucy, he was going to ask her father for her hand in marriage."

Cole paused he gave a great sigh and then continued.

"Lucy's father told Dagon to prove that he could make a living for himself and his daughter, but Dagon's company did not do so well. Turns out nobody wanted to buy fish from a weird land lover. Dagon had to watch Lucy's father marry her off to someone of more wealth."

Zindel was having a hard time putting it together.

"Dagon ran the company though. His face was on the shop, not yours."

Cole laughed at Zindel.

"We have the same face Sir Zindel. I left the area anyway

and I hear that since I have his company is doing better, but Lucy is already married. Dagon has lost her forever."

Zindel glanced over at Dagon and Morgan.

"So, the rift between you is Lucy?"

Cole looked over at them too.

"He has never come right out and said it, but I believe he blames me for losing her."

Zindel nodded before standing.

"Well Cole, you are not too strange for the company around my fire. You will be welcome anytime you are feeling too lonely."

Cole smiled at Zindel as he walked back to his sleeping quarters, thankful to have a friend.

# Chapter Eleven:

## Dameon's Decision

Dameon appeared at Mabli's window two nights after he left her. She was already asleep when he let himself in. He stood over her for a moment just watching the smile play of her lips.

"She must be having a good dream," He thought.

Dameon knelt down to kiss her on the forehead. Slowly Mabli opened her eyes. She was not startled or frightened to see him starring back at her. She just smiled and slowly sat up.

"Dameon, I was not expecting you for a few days more. No worries though I can be ready in just a few moments."

Mabli started to get up but Dameon held her there.

"It is not time to go Mabli. It will never be time to go."

Mabli pushed Dameon's hands off her.

"What do you mean? What has happened?"

Dameon looked away from her. Mabli tried to comfort him. She placed her arms around his waist.

"What is it my love? What problem have we run into? Is it Goodwin? Has he changed anybody else's mind?"

Dameon stood from the bed and turned away from her.

"No, it is not Goodwin."

Mabli had an idea where this might be leading and she fought to hold back her tears.

"Then who was it?"

Dameon sighed and turned to face her. Seeing the apology hidden in his face was enough of an answer. The tears rolled down her cheeks.

"Why?"

Dameon rushed to her side at the sight of tears, but Mabli pushed him away.

"Why? Do you not love me anymore?"

Dameon looked horrified.

"No Mabli no, It is because I love you that I can not…"

He broke off because Mabli started to sob silently. Dameon wrapped an arm around her even though she fought against him. She calmed down enough to speak again.

"You love me too much to spend eternity with me?"

Dameon whispered to her now.

"No, it's not that either Mabli."

Mabli was upset and she raised her voice slightly.

"What is it then Dameon?!"

Dameon jumped back from her at her sudden increase in volume. He listened quietly for a moment for guards, but he heard none.

"I just found out what has to happen for you to become a faerie, and I won't put you through that."

Mabli froze; even the tears on her face remained still.

"I am not afraid Dameon."

Dameon sat by her again.

"I have made the decision to become human, and I will be a Prince from another town and we will be married and human together."

Mabli frowned at that idea.

"You can not become human Dameon; you are the next King as soon as you are ready. Any male can be King here, but only you can be King there."

Dameon started to shake his head back and forth. Then he stood up and started pacing the room. Mabli remained seated in her bed.

"Tell me what is going to happen at the ceremony Dameon. Let me decide if this is what I want."

Dameon stopped and starred at her. Then he sat beside her again.

"Well, first there is dinner with the whole population of Faeries."

Mabli made a disappointed face.

"I see what you mean, dinner might be impossible."

Dameon starred at her and Mabli's face broke into a smile. Dameon smiled for a moment but continued in his serious demeanor.

"After dinner you must state that you want to be a faerie and that you want me forever as I want you."

Mabli laid her head on Dameon's shoulder.

"Another simple request, what else?"

Dameon continued uneasily.

"Then you receive my mother's blessing and my love."

Mabli smiled to herself.

"Well I always thought I would eventually have to meet your mother and I already have your love."

Dameon paused and Mabli pulled away from him.

"Don't I?"

Dameon shook his head.

"Not like this. Mabli, we have to give you our blood."

Mabli started for a moment.

"Oh…well that is still not that big of a problem. Not big enough for me to not want to be with you forever, but to satisfy my curiosity, why?"

Dameon smiled.

"Human blood is not immortal. You need Faerie blood and it has to be two of us so nobody can run around on a whim making humans into faeries."

Mabli nodded her head in understanding and Dameon continued.

"After you have accepted the blood, they make room for your wings to grow."

Mabli faltered here a little.

"What do you mean by make room?"

Dameon stood and started pacing again.

"Never mind, it is not going to happen. I never want you to feel pain Mabli, never!"

Mabli reached out and grabbed his hand.

"Tell me what make room means."

Dameon sighed.

"They have to cut you. It would be a lot more painful if they did not, but Mabli do not worry. You are not doing it."

"The hell I'm not!"

Mabli cupped her hand over her mouth the moment after the words escaped her lips. She had not meant to yell them, but Dameon was not listening to her. Dameon perked his ears and ran to the closet just in time for Mabli's bedroom door to open.

"Princess—is everything alright?"

Mabli answered him as calmly as she could.

"Yes—I was having a nightmare."

The guard took two steps toward her.

"Your face Princess, you've been crying."

Mabli quickly wiped the lingering tears from her cheeks and silently cursed the heavens for giving her a red face whenever tears leaked from her eyes.

"From my nightmare I imagine."

The guard nodded his head and started to retreat from her room.

"Goodnight Princess, if you need anything, I am right outside."

Mabli gave him a very reassuring smile and the door closed. Dameon was at her side again, Mabli turned to him in whispers.

"I am going through with it Dameon. I love you and this will be nothing compared to spending forever with you. What a small price to pay."

Dameon smiled and kissed her on the forehead.

"Are you sure? I can always become human."

Mabli sighed in annoyance.

"Then we would have to live with my father."

They both made a face of disgust and Dameon stayed with Mabli until she was asleep again. Then he quietly returned to the Realm of the Faeries to tell them that Mabli was sure and that they could continue with the preparations for the ceremony.

# Chapter Twelve:

## Finding Water

On the fourth morning, Zindel awoke in the same fashion—to the smell of breakfast and the sound of others beginning to stir. Today would be a difficult task of teaching the men how to find water on the quest because the Kingdom had its own water reserves. Short of actually venturing into the Realm of the Faeries prematurely Zindel could only tell them how to find water without having them practice the knowledge. He sat them under the shade of the tree once again and started his lesson on water hunting.

"Water is an elusive element to find. If you are not careful you can be mislead. A few facts that even faeries cannot change is that animals always know where water is. So it is important to look for tracks and not to destroy them while searching."

Braen stuck his arm up and Zindel nodded in his direction.

"Faeries will mislead us away from water?"

Zindel shook his head yes. Braen smiled to himself. Zindel tried to look away and continue his lesson, but he hesitated. Owen distracted him farther.

"Zindel, how are we going to carry water on us when we are not close to a river?"

Zindel came out of his trance and looked at Owen.

"The King is providing us with water pouches made from sheep skin. They will help to keep the water cool."

Owen looked impressed and happy. Zindel continued his lesson.

"Also lush green vegetation, swarming insects and even bird flight paths can all be indications of where the water is. Everyone must be watchful and attentive."

Zindel dismissed them to practice more with the swords and bows and arrows.

"Braen, may I speak with you a moment?"

Braen stayed behind as the others left. Zindel eyed the man suspiciously.

"Braen, why do you look for evil in everything?"

Braen was surprised by this question he remained quiet. Zindel continued to push.

"Yesterday you were determined to make me say that we will encounter evil and today you seemed happy with the idea that the faeries would lure us to our deaths. Why?!"

Braen smiled having regained his composure.

"It is just nice to know that there is no difference between them and us."

Zindel almost had to laugh.

"I cannot know what you mean. If there is a stranger among us, we offer food and shelter."

Braen smirked.

"Come now Zindel, we are not all that great. The world

is full of evil and the sooner you accept it the more prepared you are for what it will throw at you."

Zindel shook his head.

"Braen, this is why you are so consumed. You focus on all the bad and none on the good. If you could see the world the way other could, if you could open your eyes to what the world can hold for you…"

"The world made me this way Zindel! Do you not see?! Can't you see that the world is just a cold and awful place, that we must bide our time here until we die and are placed into the earth where our rotting corpses can give a little back!"

Zindel had taken a few steps back.

"What happened to you Braen? What happened to make you this way?"

Braen starred at the ground.

"Life happened, Zindel and probably a little bit of evil."

Braen walked away. Zindel watched him go; he was even more confused than when he first questioned him. Zindel lingered a while where he was before setting out to observe his men while they practiced with the weapons. As he watched, he saw, not only that Braen was not practicing but also neither was Owen. Zindel spied him sitting in the shade starring off toward the village. Zindel took a seat near him. Owen started at Zindel's sudden presence.

"Zindel, you must not sneak around like that, you should make your presence known."

Zindel smiled at him.

"On the quest dangers will not make themselves known so that you might be prepared to meet them."

Owen starred out at the village again.

"Last time I checked you were not a danger and we have not yet embarked on the quest."

Zindel was silent for a moment.

"Owen, are you unsure as to whether you wish to be here?"

Owen turned to Zindel.

"What do you mean? This is my duty to my Princess."

Zindel smiled.

"A voluntary duty; you do not have to remain if you do not wish it."

Owen was silent for a moment.

"Do you wish me to leave Zindel?"

Zindel laughed.

"No, of course not, but instead of practicing with the weapons I find you here starring at the village."

Owen laughed now.

"I do not need more practice Zindel and the village, well that is my home, and I am going to miss her...it... Wyveren."

Zindel caught Owen's slip.

"Are you serious about this girl?"

Owen looked out at Wyveren again.

"I want to be. Before this quest I was thinking about proposing marriage to her, but I have nothing to offer."

Zindel starred at him.

"You have yourself. Is that not enough?"

Owen looked at Zindel again.

"Have you never dealt with a Father? He will want to know how I am going to put food on the table and how many pounds a year I can bring in. They do not care if you love their daughters or not. They will give them to the man with the most wealth."

Zindel cocked his head.

"What does the girl care about?"

Owen was silenced; he honestly did not know how she felt about him.

"I know that she cares for me as a friend. I have never told her how I feel."

Zindel shook his head now.

"The gates are open Owen. Talk to her and come back."

Owen looked out at Wyveren again and smiled.

"If I talk to her Zindel, I may never come back."

Zindel stood to leave with a fearful thought in his head. Owen may never come back to tell her. He said nothing however and went in search of Braen who had disappeared. Braen came back into the courtyard that night. Zindel saw him go to his sleeping quarters and lay down without any supper or a fire. Zindel leaned forward and around his fire to talk to Kay.

"Do you know anything of Braen's past?"

Kay turned around to look at him.

"I heard talk of his childhood."

Zindel was silent as was Bevyn while they listened to Kay.

"They say as a little boy he lost his entire family, except his older sister, to the plague. I remember that year we lost my baby sister. Anyway, his sister took responsibility for him and she went to work in a mill during the day to buy food and lodgings for them both. Braen went with her some days and helped her out. Well one day while he was there his sister's hair got caught in one of the mills and ripped her scalp right off. Braen was sent to live in an orphanage but they say he never smiled or talked. Well you know how cruel children can be; they teased him for not talking and made fun of him for crying in his sleep. I imagine the boy was reliving his sister's death in his dreams. I hear he never made a single friend."

Zindel glanced over at the sleeping man.

"No wonder he is obsessed with evil. His life has been practically nothing else."

Kay now looked at Zindel and shook his head.

"No, that's not why. I will tell you Zindel it was no surprise to me that Braen came on this quest. Ever since he was released from the orphanage, he spoke only of black magic. Magic powerful enough to bring his family back to life."

Zindel starred at Braen with a new fear in his eyes. If Braen was seeking black magic, he would most certainly attract trouble on the quest.

# Chapter Thirteen:

# Dameon and Mabli's Escape

On any number of days, Princess Mabli could be found floating around the castle with a book in hand; for she was an avid reader and her status as Princess of Wyveren had afforded her an education. However, since their last meeting, Mabli had scarcely moved from the window she knew Dameon had disappeared from. It was fortunate that at precisely the same time King Xavier had ordered Mabli to be confined to her chambers, because nobody seemed to notice her constant attention at her bedroom window. Her father, as of late, had ordered that their meals be taken together. This, of course, was about the only time during the day when Mabli was allowed to leave her bedroom. Mabli was so lost in thought about seeing Dameon again that she did not even notice that her escorts to and from the dining hall had doubled in number. Her father brought this news to her attention.

"You might be wondering Mabli, why you have more guards than usual?"

Mabli looked about herself in shock to discover that indeed she did; however, she tried to remain indifferent to the reason.

"It is because you feel I need them Father."

The King grunted his approval to her answer.

"It is also more than that Mabli. Stocking has broken through the northern boarder of Wyveren. It is not safe for you outside the palace walls."

Xavier paused for a moment before continuing.

"I am not sure how much longer it will be safe for you inside the palace walls either."

Mabli looked up at this news and for the first time in days, thoughts of Dameon left her head.

"You really believe that Stocking will want me dead?"

Xavier gave a small nod.

"Mabli if it had been you who had the accident in the woods I would want Prince Edward dead."

Mabli faltered here.

"If it was nothing more than an accident, why would you want to claim innocent blood?"

Her father turned a shade lighter than his usual sunburned complexion.

"That is not what I am saying. If you died at King Demetrious' hands then I would want his son dead as well."

Mabli frowned.

"Prince Edward did not die at your hands, so I should be safe from harms way."

Xavier gave a sigh.

"I would feel better Mabli, if I sent you to a safer place while all this war nonsense is going on."

Mabli's eyes widened with fear that she would miss Dameon when he came back for her.

"I cannot leave!"

Xavier seemed taken aback by his daughter's sudden outburst, but then he gave a smile to her.

"It is already arranged child. You shall leave before dawn and hopefully under the cover of night you shall not be detected."

Mabli sank back into her chair and tried desperately to hide her tears from her father. After dinner, Mabli was deposited back into her room. She ran right to the window and sat to watch and wait.

"If I hear nothing by midnight I shall have to go to him. I cannot let my father take me away to who knows where!"

It was half past eleven before Mabli saw anything moving in the dark. She thought that perhaps her eyes were playing tricks on her until she saw his resilient hair gleaming in the moon light. She smiled as she opened the window to receive him.

"You have no idea how lucky we are that you have come to me tonight."

Dameon smiled at her.

"You say that every time I arrive."

Mabli's face turned grave.

"No, I mean it truly. My father had plans to send me away before the sun had even risen."

Dameon seemed to change his entire demeanor in that single moment.

"Why would he send you away? Has he found out about us Mabli?"

"No, and keep your voice down! The guards have doubled."

Dameon lowered his voice to a whisper.

"Why then?"

Mabli began to gather things that she would need with her on their trip together.

"Stocking had broken through the northern boarder and my father is afraid that King Demetrious might be after my blood."

Dameon began to help her gather her things to hurry along their progress.

"He is right to guard you so. It is very probable that King Demetrious has those exact intentions."

Mabli stopped gathering now.

"Why is it that both the men in my life think that hiding me is the answer to all problems?"

Dameon placed things into her arms now for her to pack.

"I do not wish to hide you. I wish to take you away with me so that I might make you my very pretty faerie bride."

Mabli smiled at the thought. Dameon kissed her quickly on the lips and made a movement as though to hurry her along with his arms. Dameon helped Mabli out of her bedroom window and down the tree at a little past one in the morning. They managed to make it through the courtyard without waking a single sleeping man.

# Chapter Fourteen:

# Hunting

When Zindel awoke this morning, there were only a few who had not yet risen Gwynn being among them. However, as the men assembled when the sun rose every single man was accounted for and nobody had brought their breakfast with them. Zindel took them into the King's forest for today's lesson.

"Today I will be assessing your skills at hunting. Therefore, in teams of three you will each go out and hunt until you hear me call you back. Bring your kill with you."

Zindel selected the first team to go out. Bevyn, Razial, and Tristram headed out together. Razial and Tristram headed the group and Bevyn trailed behind them. The only sounds that could be heard were Bevyn's clumsy footsteps. Razial turned his head to glance at Bevyn and the boy stopped.

"What do you hear?"

Bevyn asked excitement in his voice.

"I hear nothing but the sound of your feet lad. Try rolling

your foot from heel to toe when you walk instead of sliding them on the ground, like this."

Razial demonstrated to Bevyn the correct way to walk and the boy tried it. Razial smiled.

"There's a good lad. Let's go now shall we?"

Tristram and Bevyn nodded in agreement and they continued forward. After walking and listening for about ten minutes, Razial finally heard a rustle in the bushes around them. He very quietly turned toward it and readied his arrow when Tristram's piercing cry ruined his concentration and startled the unsuspecting rabbit. Razial turned to glance at Tristram now as anger filled his eyes and then just as quickly evaporated when he took in the scene before him. Bevyn was picking up an arrow that was a few feet ahead of him and Tristram was rubbing his backside where it was apparent that Bevyn's arrow had bounced off.

"I'm so sorry! I did not mean it. The arrow just slipped from my fingers and it was gone before I could grab it."

Tristram was giving a very sour face to Bevyn and Razial burst into laughter.

"Well Tristram, just be glad the little lad doesn't have a lot of strength yet, or we might have to bring *you* back to Zindel."

Bevyn was trying very hard not to laugh at this thought because Tristram was not yet ready to see humor in his slightly injured backside. He turned very seriously to both Bevyn and Razial.

"We tell no one about this…do you understand?!"

Bevyn nodded very seriously and Razial chuckled it off.

"Very well Tristram. Shall we continue? After you Bevyn."

Bevyn sauntered forward and Tristram gave a silent smile

to himself. After about a half an hour of being out in the forest Zindel called them back. Bevyn had no kill with him, Tristram had a rabbit but the animal had so many arrows in it that by the time they were all removed there was barely enough meat for one of the dwarves to be filled on. Razial however brought back three rabbit and two quail. Zindel swelled with pride, and this was only the first team.

Gwynn, Braen, and Erwin left in the same direction as the first three. Gwynn was twirling his long radiant hair between his fingers while he followed the dark one and the light one as he called them. Gwynn was not much for friends at all, but if he had to pick between them he would definitely choose the light one. Erwin suddenly turned to face them.

"Do you suppose that if we fail this test Zindel will send us home?"

Braen turned his head quickly toward those he had been ignoring only moments ago. He had not considered that possibility. Of course, everybody had to be useful to go on the quest—and he was not much of a fighter. He had to be on this quest though. Braen started taking off in a new direction. Erwin starred after him.

"Where are you going?"

Braen answered solemnly.

"I am not hunting the same area the others did. Did you see how much they brought back? There will be nothing left."

Gwynn spoke again as they started to follow.

"I would not worry about it. Zindel has to ask the King permission before he dismisses anyone, and well lets just say that the King will want any extra men to help Zindel; besides the child did not return with anything."

Erwin relaxed for a bit and then Braen spoke again.

"'The Child' is Zindel's squire now—he gets special treatment. Do not think the King will have any influence with Zindel either. Do you not know Zindel's record of accomplishment? He does what he wants and takes the punishment for it later."

Erwin was starting to get anxious; he did not want to be left behind. Braen was getting further and further ahead and Gwynn was falling further and further behind. Erwin decided to stop and wait for Gwynn then they would both catch up to Braen. Erwin actually had to walk backwards to Gwynn after waiting several minutes and found him sitting on a fallen tree trying to untangle leaves and twigs from his hair. Erwin stood next to him.

"Come friend, we must catch up to Braen."

Gwynn gave a scowl in his direction.

"If you are a friend, help me to free my hair from this evil!"

Erwin laughed.

"This 'evil' is nature and there is no point in getting it out now. Wait until we are free from this test."

Gwynn raised his voice now.

"I refuse to move from this tree until I am decent!"

They both heard rustling in the bushes. Gwynn covered his face with his hands and Erin readied his bow, pointing at the direction of the sound. Braen suddenly popped out. He stopped, startled for a moment. Erwin sighed and lowered his bow. Braen starred at the two men for a moment.

"I saw the signal. Zindel is calling us back."

Erwin sighed again upset.

"Oh great and we have nothing to show."

Braen smiled to himself.

"I wouldn't say nothing."

Again, after about a half an hour's time Zindel called them back. Gwynn came back with leaves and roots in his hair.

"This is why we buy our meat from the butcher!"

Zindel had to laugh at this disheveled form of disobedience. Braen came back with a quail, but it was a young one. It looked young enough to still be following its mother. Zindel took the small bird from Braen's hand. It had no arrow wound, but its neck was broken. Braen had caught and killed the baby bird with his bare hands. Zindel did not say a word to Braen, just handed him back the dead baby quail. Erwin came back without anything either. Zindel sent Kay, Owen, and Awstin next. He hoped that somebody from this group bring something back. They decided to head in the opposite direction of the first team and inadvertently in the same direction as the second team. They assumed, like the second team, that the first group had gotten all there was to get. However, they did not realize that the second team had such poor luck in the same area they were directly heading. Awstin passed by a patch of sunlight and just stood there and closed his eyes for a moment and smiled. Kay, who was walking in front of him, turned at the sudden absent sound of his footsteps.

"Come Awstin, now is not the time for sleep."

Awstin's eyes popped open and he continued forward.

"I was not sleeping, I was remembering."

Kay huffed in response.

"It looked like sleep to me, you even had a dreamers smile on your face."

Awstin smiled to himself.

"I told you, I was remembering…her."

Both Kay and Owen stopped to turn and look at him.

"Her who?" They asked in unison.

Awstin smiled again.

"I do not know. She haunts my dreams. I always find her singing in a stream of sunlight—just like that one. She always recognizes me, but I have no inclination as to who she is."

Owen raised an eyebrow.

"She is not a young maiden from the village then?"

Awstin shook his head.

"I have searched every face for her here, believe me."

Kay ventured a guess.

"Perhaps it is the Princess? She hardly ever comes to the village. Maybe you saw her once and she left an impression."

Awstin shook his head, but slower.

"I do not think so. This girl in my dreams would not be so cruel as to let me glimpse my happiness with someone who could never be."

Owen smiled deeply again.

"Princess Mabli currently has no suitor. Who is to say it is a happiness that could never be."

Awstin's face made an expression of understanding and excitement before Kay spoke again.

"You forget Owen, Princesses marry Princes—not village men."

Awstin's face fell again but not as it had fallen before, he had never thought of Princess Mabli because he was a village man and not a Prince. However, he was going on a quest, which would make him knightly if they succeeded—and he would be saving her life. It was a possibility that his dream girl was Princess Mabli and it thrilled him. Awstin could not wait to fall asleep again and study her face, to remember it—though he was sure that he could pick it out of a crowd if he had too. Kay grumbled to the others.

"Lets stop scaring everything away now shall we?"

The three continued to hunt until their time was up. Once Zindel called them back, Kay emerged first and his hands were empty. Awstin came back next and he carried a rabbit with him. Zindel smiled as Owen came back last, carrying two rabbits. Cole, Dagon and Morgan were next to go out. Zindel hoped that by grouping them together they would start talking. They walked into the woods more for show than hunting. Dagon and Morgan were engrossed with conversation about how their business when the people learned that both owners had helped to save the Princesses life. Cole was deep in thought about the quest. He desperately wanted to go but hunting was not going to be his thing. Just thinking about all the animals back at the camp already was intimidating. How was he going to pull his weight? Cole stooped down to pick up a stick. It was a good size stick, perfect for poking fires with. Then he found another one, it was also perfect so he picked it up too. Cole had about ten sticks before Dagon or Morgan noticed him. Morgan cocked his head and Dagon lifted an eyebrow.

"Have you gone completely mad? Do you eat trees as well as live in them?"

Cole turned a very red color as he tuned to look at his brother and former childhood friend.

"Well, no. Let us not kid ourselves though. Us…hunt… is that not completely mad?"

They looked at each other and then back at Cole.

"So what are you doing then? I think Zindel will be much more displeased if we show up with sticks than nothing."

Cole placed his sticks down so he could talk with his hands.

"I disagree. We cannot hunt, but so what. Look at

everything out there already. They don't need more hunters on this quest, but we don't have any gatherers."

Dagon and Morgan finally understood. If they wanted to make themselves useful to the quest, they had to do what nobody else had yet. Morgan turned to face Cole.

"Good thinking Cole, really".

Cole resumed picking up his sticks and Dagon helped him. Dagon starred at Cole and looked like he wanted to say something to him but did not. Morgan started to pick up rocks since the other two had the sticks covered. After about the same time as the rest he called them back. Morgan came back first and he had his arms full of large stones. Shortly afterwards Cole and Dagon appeared both of their little arms were full of wood. Zindel was perplexed.

"Do you suppose that you can eat these things?"

Cole was quick to respond.

"No, Sir Zindel, but we should cook the meat that has already been caught."

Zindel looked from one dwarf to the next.

"Your assignment was to hunt."

Morgan commented now.

"And so we did."

Zindel repeated himself.

"Your assignment was to hunt animals."

Dagon dropped his armload of wood.

"We tried that Zindel, but we are fisherman. Put us on a lake and watch the fish jump in our boat but don't expect birds to fly onto our arrows."

Zindel nodded, they were being honest. Zindel had not expected any meat to return with them anyway. He called forth the last group of men, Seith, Trent, and Kyle. Zindel held out high hopes for them. They took off right away in the direction of the first group. There was very little spoken between any of the men. The only sound heard was the pluck of the string as the arrow was released. Trent and Kyle were the only ones to hit anything, but Seith did not mind. He had just as much fun trying. All three of the men were just settling down and gathering their kills when they heard the rustling in the bushes. Trent and Kyle looked at each other in recognition.

"Do you think we are allowed to hunt that?"

Trent asked with a smile. Kyle responded.

"Zindel just said to hunt, he didn't say what."

Seith starred at them both as they took off after the animal. He tried to keep up, but both of the others left their kills behind in their current pursuit. Seith could not carry everything and keep pace with them. He decided to sit down and wait. He heard the animal fighting back and more than anything he felt he should be there to help. Then there was silence. Seith waited anxiously for one of them to come and get him, or to tell him to run for help. As he waited, he saw Zindel's signal to return to camp. He would not return—not yet, not without his whole party. There was a rustling sound. Seith turned his head and starred when Trent came through. Seith jumped up when he saw him.

"Is everything okay? Should I go and…"

Seith was stunned into silence as Kyle came through and between the brothers was their kill. Kyle flashed a toothy smile.

"Hey Seith, I forgot you were with us. Great now you can carry everything else."

They slowly made their way back to Zindel. When Zindel did called them back after a half an hour's time all three men came back carrying something. Seith was carrying three rabbit and three quail. Zindel smiled at him.

"Seith you are a secret hunter!"

Seith dropped these kills on top of all the others.

"Oh no Zindel, none of those were mine."

Zindel looked confused until he saw both Kyle and Trent walking towards him. They held a large male pig between them. The men sat in awe while they watched Kyle and Trent lay the pig next to the fire that Kay had started.

# Chapter Fifteen:

## Dameon and Mabli's Journey

Dameon and Mabli arrived in the Realm of the Faeries just as the sun was rising. Mabli paused to see knights hiking toward them. Dameon pulled her along.

"They should not see you."

Mabli nodded.

"I know that, but I am curious as to why they are here instead of fighting the war. Maybe it is over Dameon!"

Dameon chuckled at his sweet naïve bride to be.

"I doubt that. You said that Stocking broke through the northern boarder. I imagine the knights have orders to move in and guard the town boarders now."

They walked on until they came to a tree, which Dameon spoke too. Mabli had never been this far into the Realm of the Faeries; she looked more closely to see a pair of eyes on the tree. Mabli, startled by this, gave a small gasp and cupped her hand to her mouth to stifle the noise. Dameon laughed at her.

"Jeanie show yourself to your future Queen."

Suddenly where the tree was a beautiful, tall, slender faerie appeared. She had long, golden hair with green eyes and huge, butterfly like wings which were also green.

"Hello future Queen, sorry to startle you."

Mabli curtsied to Jeanie but could not say a word for she was awestruck. Jeanie moved a tree branch and the trunk of the tree opened up. Mabli now focused her attention on that. Dameon led her down the steps that were revealed by the opening of the trunk. They walked for what seemed like days on this underground passage; however, it was only a matter of hours until they came to a second set of steps leading upward again. Dameon placed his family pendent into the lock and the door sprang open. Mabli glanced around at what appeared to be an ice cave, though it had all the comforts of home. Dameon took Mabli's hand and ushered her toward a throne where the most beautiful faerie Mabli had ever seen was sitting. She had shoulder length brown hair and hazily green eyes; her skin was as creamy white as the dress she wore and she had a warm friendly smile. Dameon spoke.

"Mother, may I introduce Princess Mabli of Wyveren."

Mabli faltered slightly. Dameon could have mentioned that she was to be meeting his mother first thing. Mabli made a deep bow, but the pretty faerie picked her up off the floor.

"Mabli my dear, here we greet one another face to face."

Mabli smiled and embraced her mother-in-law to be.

"Thank you for your gracious welcome Ms…" Mabli was at a loss, she had never enquired as to what Dameon's Mothers name was. The pretty faerie smiled at her still.

"My name is Tessah, but I insist that you call me Mom."

Mabli smiled and nodded as Tessah went on to speak.

"Now, the first thing you children shall do is go to sleep and refresh for this evening's ceremony."

Tessah stared off in a single direction for a moment. Not two seconds later two faeries dressed in a matching uniform appeared.

"You called Queen Tessah?"

She smiled at them.

"Please show Princess Mabli of Wyveren to her room and attend to her every wish."

The matching faeries took Mabli's bags from Prince Dameon and Mabli herself and walked down a hallway. Mabli followed them as Dameon went to his own chambers.

# Chapter Sixteen:

## Skinning, Gutting and Cooking

Seith sat down next to the pile of animals and started to skin one of the rabbits. Braen joined him and took far too much joy in taking the skin off the animals. Awstin also volunteered to this tedious task along with Zindel and Bevyn. Zindel spoke.

"Seith you are very skilled at this. Look Bevyn he can skin a whole rabbit and lay it out as one piece."

Seith smiled.

"Yes, my family is made up of sheep herders. We do a lot of skinning. My father taught me how to do this as he did all of my brothers."

Zindel's curiosity was peaked.

"How many siblings do you have?"

Seith was silent for a moment as though counting in his head.

"Well, let me put it this way. I am the seventh child born in my family and one of the middle children at that."

Zindel was completely shocked.

"How did your parents feel about your leaving?"

Seith smiled to himself.

"I am not even sure they know I am gone. However, if they do then they count it as a blessing for it is one less mouth to feed."

They all laughed along with him at this. After the rabbits, quails, and pig were skinned, Tristram came over. Zindel eyed him as he sat down.

"You've missed the skinning Tristram."

Tristram smiled at Zindel as he picked up a rabbit.

"Good thing too, I hate skinning."

Tristram pierced the belly of the rabbit with his sword and gutted it with everybody watching. The men, especially Braen, watched intently and then tried to copy him. Zindel talked to him while they worked.

"Let me guess, you come from a family of butchers."

Tristram paused in his gutting to look up at Zindel.

"My father runs the butcher shop in town, yes."

Zindel went back to his gutting.

"Well, he taught you well."

Tristram faltered.

"My father taught me nothing. I learned how these men are learning now; careful observation from a distance."

Zindel frowned.

"Why wouldn't your father teach you the family business? You are

going to take it over one day aren't you?"

Tristram now seemed to gut more viciously than before.

"I think my father resented me for being born."

Zindel thought that was an awful thing to say, but from what he was learning from these men, it was probably true. Tristram continued to talk.

"Neither my mother or father asked me to stay home."

Zindel silently wondered why, but he was determined not to ask for the subject seemed to pain him. Bevyn was not as perceptive however.

"My mother begged me to stay! With father gone fighting the war she is all alone."

Tristram continued to gut, but did steal a glance at the boy.

"Well then feel lucky that you are wanted."

Bevyn went to comment back but Zindel silenced him with a glare. Razial was sitting close to the fire where all the men were skinning and gutting their kills for the day, just listening to them talk and watching them work. Suddenly Kay came into Razial's sight and Razial turned his focus to this man, who knew him—who lived next door to him all this time and who Razial never even looked at twice before this quest. He was always too engrossed in his own sorrow to notice anybody else. He watched as Kay tended to the fire as though it was his child. As Razial sat watching Kay give more attention to this fire than he himself even gave to his parents, he was reminded of a story he had heard when he was just married to his young wife.

"Kay, I was just sitting here thinking to myself that you remind me of a story I heard about sixteen years ago."

Kay and all the rest of the men momentarily stopped what they were doing to listen. Kay's interest was peaked.

"What story is that?"

Razial smiled as he began his tail.

"About sixteen years ago we had one of the worst winters

in Wyveren. A blizzard struck in the middle of the day and we could not leave our houses. When the blizzard subsided, we all came out of our houses realizing the children were still in school and that they were snowed in. Therefore, we hurried to the school and started digging, already knowing that we would be too late for all the firewood was still outside. When we finally got the snow cleared enough to open the door it was as warm as a chimney in that little room. The teacher was crying and all the children were huddled up around the fire place where they were burning the desks."

Kay smile at Razial.

"That's a lovely story. I am glad the teacher had enough sense to burn the desks instead of letting the children and she freeze to death."

Razial smiled wider now.

"I never said the teacher was a woman, but you know because you were the boy who started the fire and saved everyone's life."

All the men turned to look at Kay now. A deep blush rose in his cheeks.

"I...no it...it was Miss Gable who--"

Razial kept on smiling.

"I certainly did not say the teacher's name."

Kay stared dumbly at all the men starring at him.

"All right, I am the boy. Poor Miss Gable tried her best, but she could not get a flame going."

Razial smiled, pleased with himself at least of knowing the man who was his neighbor all these years, even if it was a story from his childhood. Erwin came to the group of skinners and gutters now. Bevyn glace up at him.

"You are too late. You have missed the skinning and the gutting."

Erwin smiled at the boy.

"Those are not my areas of expertise young lad."

Zindel watched as Erwin loaded the quails and the rabbits onto sturdy sticks he had found and shaped in the forest. Zindel walked over to the fire to observe Erwin as he worked. Erwin noticed him.

"Yes I am a baker."

Zindel smiled at him.

"That was easy to conclude. You handle your cooking extremely well. I am curious as to where you and your family come from."

Erwin's eyes looked up at Zindel, but the rest of his body continued to cook the animals.

"I come from Wyveren like the rest."

Zindel chuckled.

"I am not trying to make you an outcast Erwin, but you are different from these men."

Erwin grimaced.

"I am no different."

Zindel pointed to the men who were butchering the pig. Then he pointed to the dwarves and the rest of the men who were talking amongst themselves around the same fire that Erwin was cooking.

"Everybody else had reddened in the sun. Everybody else has scrapes and bruises from our exercises and lessons. You, Erwin, are different from the rest."

Erwin looked back at the fire and realized he was letting one of the quail burn. Zindel question him again.

"Where is it that you come from?"

Erwin whispered now.

"I do not know sir Zindel. I was left on the doorstep of

the people I call family. They took me in and raised me as their own."

Zindel smiled to himself. He pressed the issue no further. The men dined on quail, rabbit, and pig for lunch that day and Zindel led them out of the forest afterwards to spend the rest of the day practicing with the weapons. To lift the men's spirits he held a competition for the best swordsman. In the first round, all the men battled against one partner. The loser of that battle became the audience and then the winners battled against each other. This cycled down until only Owen and Zindel remained. Their sword fight was something that should have been written about. The men had never seen swords fly that fast before. Finally, it ended and Zindel was the victor.

# Chapter Seventeen:

## Zindel's Request To The King

Zindel returned to King Xavier's throne that night. Xavier was feasting on an entire turkey by himself. He waved his turkey leg at Zindel as he entered the room.

"I hear that some of your men managed to catch a boar in my forest today."

Zindel nodded, Xavier continued.

"So the training is going well then?"

Zindel smiled at the King.

"Some of the men have exceeded my expectations."

The King drank deeply from his goblet.

"I am happy to hear that Zindel."

Zindel paused for a moment before speaking his mind.

"My Lord, there are three men I wish to leave behind."

Xavier starred at Zindel for a long moment.

"Who are they and why do you wish it?"

Zindel swallowed.

"The first man is Braen. He disturbs me Sire. He killed a baby quail today with his bare hands. I feel that he will attract unnecessary trouble and evil on our journey."

Xavier had gone back to picking at his plate of food. He answered after popping a grape into his mouth.

"Listen to me Zindel sometimes you need a man like that. Someone who will do what nobody else can."

Zindel pleaded further.

"Sire, I doubt greatly that he will risk anything for anybody out there."

Zindel was pointing toward the courtyard where his men were enjoying their dinner. The King smiled at him.

"If anything, perhaps he will make a good distraction for a safe getaway. He shall go Zindel."

Zindel furrowed his eyebrows at Xavier's suggestion but continued.

"The next man I wish to leave is Gwynn."

Xavier peered at Zindel with his eyes squinted and his head cocked.

"The handsome one? Who is always flipping his hair?"

Zindel nodded; slightly surprised that King Xavier knew who his men were.

"He has shown no useful skills and he does not listen to orders, My Lord."

The King chuckled at this.

"Ah Zindel, he must go with you."

Zindel's jaw dropped for a brief second.

"He is of no use to me Sire."

Xavier now peeled the skin off his turkey leg and gobbled up the fatty flavor before speaking.

"He is Zindel. He will keep you on your toes—keep you from becoming too soft. You must remain cold and distant when dealing with Faeries. Reveal nothing and they can take nothing. Besides you might even find that he has skills yet."

Zindel forgot for a moment that he was in the presence of the King.

"That man's only skill is primping!"

Xavier laughed at hearty laugh at Zindel's folly.

"If nothing else Zindel, you may use him for a distraction for a safe getaway."

Zindel faltered here.

"Are you telling me to bring these men to sacrifice them?"

Xavier ignored Zindel's question.

"Who is the third you wish to leave?"

Zindel shifted his weight, he was not going to let the previous question be forgotten, but for now, he had to answer his King.

"I wish to leave Bevyn."

The King stopped his eating now, which meant he was truly surprised.

"Isn't that your squire?"

Zindel glanced at the floor.

"Yes My Lord."

Xavier resumed his eating.

"Why do you wish to leave him?"

Zindel sighed.

"He is not as advanced as I would like him to be. It would be more of a chore to bring him along. I would have to watch him more closely than any of the others…"

At that moment there was a clattering sound behind the doorway from which Zindel had entered. He quickly drew his sword and headed in that direction. However, about a foot away, one of the servants came through it with a tray. Upon the tray sat a goblet, a mountain of food and an upset bottle of wine.

"What happened?!"

Zindel demanded. The servant shook his head.

"Somebody bumped into me, but I could not see who over the tray."

Zindel looked down the hallway but saw no one. He returned to Xavier. He was holding his goblet out to be refilled by what was left in the bottle. Zindel continued his plea to leave Bevyn behind.

"Also Sire, I do not wish anything to happen to the boy. This is a very dangerous quest and I will not be able to protect my men properly with my constant attention and worry on Bevyn."

Xavier had downed his goblet while Zindel was speaking and now he looked at Zindel with a bit of a drunken eye.

"Your squire will go with you Zindel. You will continue your training with him."

Zindel started to argue but Xavier silenced him.

"I know, he is not where you would like him to be—but that is preciously why you need to take him with you. Ever since the war started all the squires have been put on hold; at this point there will be no knights left to train them."

Zindel ached to hear news of the war.

"What news do you have from the front lines?"

Xavier began to speak loosely.

"Stocking has broken through the northern boarder of Wyveren."

Zindel's face all at once became determined and Xavier

realized his blunder immediately. He quickly added to his earlier statement.

"Our knights have held them at bay so far. I have thought of sending more knights to help defend, but that would leave a gap and an easy breach point for Stocking."

Xavier looked up and saw that Zindel was still looking determined to return to the war as soon as their conversation was done.

"Do not worry yourself with the war Zindel. Your job is to find the Golden Staff of Enchantment for your Princess!"

Zindel nodded his head with a heavy heart.

"My Lord, do you have an answer for my question earlier?"

Xavier lifted his head.

"You mean about the sacrificing? Call it what you wish Zindel, it is all the same. Leave one man to save the rest."

Zindel was disgusted with the idea of it.

"I could never do that my King."

Xavier chuckled.

"You can and you will. You are dismissed Zindel."

Zindel left the room and a messenger came running up to the King. Xavier grunted his acknowledgement to him.

"Sire...it is Princess Mabli. She is...she has..."

Xavier finally turned his head and spoke to the man.

"Spit it out! What of my daughter?"

The messenger wiped away the bits of food that had flown onto his face from the King's mouth.

"She is not in her room, Sire. Nobody knows where she has gone."

Xavier was stunned slightly. He knew not which actions to take. Obviously, Stocking had somehow managed to grab her.

"Did they get her while she was traveling away from Wyveren?"

The messenger started to stutter again.

"N…no…no Sire. She never got in the carriage. She was taken from her chambers."

Xavier's eyes were wide now.

"Stocking has men in my Palace?! Hold all the guards that were on watch of Mabli. Take them to the dungeons! We will find out what they have done with her!"

Zindel returned to his men at their fires. Kay sat around Zindel's fire, but Bevyn was nowhere to be found.

"Kay, where is the little lad?"

Kay looked up.

"Last he told me, he had gone to find you."

Kay started to look around him and spotted him beside Cole.

"He must have gotten side tracked."

Zindel released a sigh of relief. For a moment, he thought the little lad might have heard his request.

# Chapter Eighteen:

## Faerie Facts

When Zindel awoke the next morning, Bevyn had already prepared breakfast for the both of them and was going around waking up the other men. Zindel waited until the boy came back to start eating. Bevyn did not look Zindel directly in the eye, but other than that, it was as though nothing had changed between them.

"Is there something wrong with your breakfast Sir Zindel?"

Zindel shook his head.

"No little lad, I was just waiting for you so we might enjoy this fine feast together."

Bevyn smiled to himself under Zindel's praise. Kay and Cole soon joined them.

As soon as the sun had risen and the men assembled Zindel led them once again to the shade of the trees in the King's courtyard. The men seated themselves facing the rock, which Zindel took a seat upon.

"Today," Zindel started, "I am going to talk to you about the faeries."

Braen's hand shot up. Zindel nodded in his direction.

"Are you also going to talk about the evil spirits you mentioned the other day?"

Zindel sighed.

"Perhaps, if we have time after we have talked about the faeries."

Braen again raised his hand but did not wait for permission to speak.

"It is the evil spirits that are a threat to us. Not the faeries."

Zindel cocked his head.

"What makes you say that?"

Braen chuckled.

"Honestly Zindel, the most faeries can do is steal your food if you leave it out. I know because I have had it happen to me on many a Friday."

Braen of course was referring to the last Friday of every moon when the faeries were known to venture out of their world and wander into the homes of the townspeople. If any food was left out, they would eat it. It was customary in the village to leave food and water out to welcome the faeries into their homes because a faerie was an omen of good luck. Zindel now spoke above the laughter of the men agreeing with Braen.

"Faeries, no matter how innocent they seem are dangerous."

Gwynn tossed his hair for there was no wind to do it for him.

"How can faeries be dangerous? They won't even eat whole foods."

This was also true and also why if there was anything that you did not want the faeries to eat you were suppose to put a hole in the middle of it or break it into pieces. Zindel waited for the men to quiet down.

"The reason this quest is so dangerous is because faeries try to lure men into their world. If you go with them, well it is safe to say that nobody who has gone missing has ever returned to the people who know him."

Awstin raised his hand now.

"Does anybody know what the faeries do with the men?"

Zindel answered without hesitation.

"According to legend there is only one male faerie able to mate at a time. He is the King of the Faeries. However even he is only able to mate until a male heir is born. So in order to keep the race going faeries will take human men to mate with them."

Zindel could hear that the men did not seem to think that this was so terrible a crime. Trent elbowed Kyle as he laughed.

"I wish all females were like the faeries little brother; just a romp in the woods and then no more fuss or flowers or meeting the parents."

The men burst into laughter and Kyle retorted once it had died down.

"Tell that to young Bevyn, he is not even aware of women yet!"

Bevyn felt the heat rise in his face and he smiled sheepishly as the crowd laughed around him.

"I am aware of some."

He cried in his defense. Awstin questioned further.

"So there are only two male faeries at a time?"

Zindel was brought back to the point of this conversation now.

"No, not at all you see faeries are immortal. So all the male faeries have been King at one point, but they cannot reproduce."

Awstin was openly questioning now.

"So what would happen if one of the faeries mates with a human and births a male?"

Zindel flicked his eyes for just a moment in Erwin's direction.

"The male babe is stripped of his wings at birth and left in the village of his father."

Erwin's hand shot up now. Zindel acknowledged him.

"So the faeries just return the men to their village once they have mated?"

Zindel shook his head.

"No, the man is released into a different part of the world with no memory of who he is or where he comes from."

Erwin looked disheartened at this news. Braen paid no mind to the quiet moment that passed between them and he spoke freely without permission.

"Okay, so faeries can do more than steal food, but honestly if you have nothing to keep you in Wyveren then the worst they can do to you is give you a good lay."

Erwin silently glared at Braen and Zindel responded.

"If you have nothing to keep you in Wyveren and you would not mind losing all of your memories then I suppose you have nothing to fear from the faeries. However there are more than just faeries out there."

Braen leaned back with his arms crossed as though daring Zindel to contradict him. Zindel took his gaze away from Braen and moved it to the other men.

"There are witches and werewolves out there. Not to mention, faerie experiments, which are unpredictable at times; there are spells and entrapments we will walk into."

The men were silent. Braen challenged Zindel no further. After some more questions and answers, Zindel dismissed the men for their mid-day meal. It was at this time a guard came down from the palace to summon Zindel.

"Sir Zindel, King Xavier is asking for you."

Zindel followed the guard to Xavier's throne. He was also eating his lunch. The moment he saw Zindel approaching, Xavier slammed his food upon the plate and grabbed a gold linen napkin to wipe the grease from his hands and face.

"Why are you still here Zindel?!"

Zindel was slightly taken aback. The King kept ranting at him.

"I expected you to be gone before the first morning light!"

Zindel was now allowed to speak.

"Sire, we are leaving tomorrow before the first morning light. This is our seventh and final day of training."

The King erupted here.

"You are my most advanced Knight and yet you can not do simple arithmetic! This is your eighth day of training Zindel!"

Zindel calmly counted in his head, he was sure he was not wrong.

"Good King, forgive me, but I am counting seven days since I brought the men here, only seven days since they started their training."

Xavier resumed eating.

"I have seen your miscalculation Zindel. You seemed to have assumed I meant you could have seven days to train the men once you found them. The same day I gave you the order counted as day one."

Zindel's face fell.

"King Xavier there is still much to go over with these men. I need this other half of the day to complete their training."

King Xavier looked into his goblet and saw that it was empty. He snapped his short portly fingers and a servant came with a bottle of wine.

"Well, you shall have to complete your training on the quest. Your men and you shall leave immediately."

Zindel stood in front of the King completely shocked. Xavier glanced up at Zindel and noticed he was still standing there.

"You are dismissed."

Zindel had no choice but to turn around and get his men ready to leave immediately.

# Chapter Nineteen:

## The Ceremony

When Mabli awoke, she felt very refreshed. Mabli glanced around her very large room and noticed a small circular pool toward the window. She walked over to it and a servant appeared.

"Might I prepare the water for a bath Princess Mabli?"

Mabli nodded her head yes and watched as the faerie touch his finger to the water. The moment he did the water started to bubble. The servant turned toward Mabli now.

"You will find the water quite to your liking Princess. I shall lay out a dress for you and then see myself out. Simply call out when you are ready to return to the company of the Queen and Prince Dameon."

Mabli nodded again for she was too shy to speak. As soon as the servant left the room, Mabli stripped of her traveling dress and dipped herself into the pool. It was the perfect temperature and the water was scented with lavender. Mabli emerged some time later and found that the water evaporated from her skin and hair the moment she left the water. She walked over to the dress that the servant had laid out for her. As soon as she picked up the fabric, it slipped from her fingers. The dress was so smooth that it felt like water. Mabli put it on and still felt as though she wore nothing. She looked at her reflection in the mirror and admired how she looked in the dress. It was a very light shade of purple and it hugged her curves as though it was made for her. As Mabli turned around to look at the back of the dress, she noticed two very large gaps in the fabric precisely where her shoulder blades were. Mabli arranged her hair so that it covered the missing pieces and softly said to herself that she was ready. A knock at the door that immediately followed. Mabli opened it and the servant was standing there.

"I heard you say that you were ready Princess."

Mabli nodded her head yes and the servant continued.

"Perfect timing, everyone was just sitting down to dinner."

The servant started walking and Mabli followed him. Mabli's jaw dropped as she came upon the dinning room. It was larger than the entire town of Wyveren and every Faerie in the world seemed to be dining here this evening. The servant led Mabli to the table facing every other one and sat her on the right hand side of the Queen. Dameon sat on her left and two girls sat on either side of them. The girl who sat next to Dameon wore a white dress and had lovely strawberry blonde straight hair that sat even with her chin. Her eyes were a mix between green and brown, like the Queens. The girl who sat next to Mabli had wild curly brown hair, which appeared to sit on her shoulders. She had blue eyes that appeared to match Dameon's. They both smiled warmly at Mabli. Everybody else had started to eat already so

Mabli started also for she was ravenous because she had not finished her last meal with her father. She dined on rabbit and potatoes that appeared to be smashed in her plate. They had a magnificent flavor that danced on Mabli's taste buds. The girl who sat next to her appeared to be watching her every move. No sooner than Mabli had eaten a few bites than the girl cried out with a huge smile on her face.

"Raise your hands!"

Both of Mabli's hands rose into the air. Mabli was shocked and embarrassed by her actions, which she could not seem to control. The girl sitting next to Dameon furrowed her eyebrows.

"Honestly Wilhamenia, as if the poor girl isn't frightened enough. Princess Mabli, you may lower your hands."

Mabli's hands began to come down. Wilhamenia laughed.

"Sorry Princess, just having some fun with my new sister."

Mabli smiled at her uneasily and then turned her head toward Queen Tessah.

"How is it that you can control me like that?"

The girl sitting next to Dameon answered.

"It is the food. This food was caught in the Realm of the Faeries. Therefore anybody who eats it and is not a faerie is under our control."

Mabli nodded, the girl reached around her brother and her mother to extend her hand. Mabli took it.

"My name is Esabella and I am very happy that you will be joining our family."

They chatted happily amongst themselves for the remainder of the meal. After dinner, the party moved into another room, theater style. Every Faerie there took a seat facing the stage and the Queen, Dameon, and Mabli stepped onto the stage. Each of them took a seat in the chairs placed up there for them. A servant soon came with three empty glasses and placed one empty glass in front of each person. Queen Tessah spoke loudly for the entire audience to hear.

"Princess Mabli, human, from Wyveren, you come before us in the Realm of the Faeries asking to become a faerie yourself?"

Mabli realized she was supposed to answer.

"Yes."

The Queen smiled at her.

"Speak up my dear, they all must hear you."

Mabli blushed slightly, but raised her voice.

"Yes I wish to become a faerie."

The other faeries clapped and cheered. When they settled down the Queen continued.

"Into this glass I pour my blessing."

The Queen took a sharp knife from the servant who just appeared, sliced a long line across her hand, and let the blood fall into her glass. Mabli was very alarmed and started slightly. Dameon placed a hand upon her shoulder and smiled at her. The Queen began to speak again.

"Dameon, Prince in the Realm of the Faeries, is it your wish to give Princess Mabli the girt of eternal life in the Realm of the Faeries?"

Dameon stood.

"It is my wish!"

The Queen continued.

"Is it also your wish to share your life and your love with Princess Mabli for all eternity?"

Dameon looked back at Mabli.

"That is also my wish!"

The crowd erupted in cheer. As they quieted, Queen Tessah passed the knife to her son.

"Fill your cup with your love."

Dameon ripped his shirt open, drove the knife into his heart, and let the blood pour forth into his cup. Mabli had her hands to her mouth to prevent a scream escaping her lips. Then Queen Tessah and Prince Dameon brought their glasses together and poured all of its contents into Mabli's glass. She stared at it trying to keep her face from looking disgusted. The Queen turned to the audience.

"Princess Mabli will now accept the offering of love from Prince Dameon and my blessing!"

The audience waited in silence and all eyes were upon Princess Mabli. She was wishing she were still as ravenous as before. She grabbed the glass and tipped it into her throat. She finished the glass in one breath and the audience cheered. Two servants came, lifted Princess Mabli from her chair, and turned her around so that her back was facing the audience. One of them moved her hair and then they both held her steady. Mabli was slightly alarmed and then she heard Queen Tessah.

"With the acceptance of love and blessing may your wings grow proud and true!"

At the end of this statement, Mabli cried out with agonizing pain as the knife pierced her skin. The Queen made deep cuts in Mabli's back where the fabric was missing.

"Where the skin has parted, allow the wings through!"

The Queen cried to the crowd and they cheered louder than ever. Mabli was turned around to face them with tears streaming down her face. The Queen turned to face Dameon and Mabli.

"A kiss will complete the ceremony."

Dameon pulled Mabli close to him, careful to avoid her new lacerations and deeply and passionately kissed her. The audience cheered repeatedly. All three of them stepped off the stage and into the wings where healers were waiting. They went to work straight away on Tessah and Dameon. Dameon spoke to Mabli.

"I am sorry my love, but your wounds must heal naturally."

Mabli nodded with a smile, but felt as though she would faint from the pain. Tessah spoke as her hand was healed.

"Servants, take Mabli to her chambers. You will feel better dear over the next couple of weeks."

Mabli started here.

"Weeks, I cannot be away that long! Already my father must know that I am missing. I am sure he is full of worry for my safety. I must return to Wyveren as soon as possible."

The Queen was uneasy at this.

"Mabli my dear, stay with us. This is where you will be living for all time. Leave your old life and your father behind you."

Mabli kneeled before the Queen.

"Mom, you do not understand. The war that exists between Stocking and Wyveren is growing worse. My father had plans to send me away because he feared for my safety. I feel sure that he will blame Stocking for my disappearance and make ending the war completely impossible. Now I know that the war does not directly involve the Faeries, but how long until it does? Let me go back to my father and perhaps this war can end before my wings grow in."

The Queen looked grave. She turned to her son.

"Dameon, what do you feel about it?"

Dameon grimaced.

"I feel we should have left your father a note."

Mabli nodded in agreement.

"Looking back now that is the obvious choice, but we left in such a hurry I am afraid my mind was not thinking of the consequences of my actions."

It was agreed that Mabli would return to Wyveren the next day to alert her father that she was live and well, and once she was recovered enough she would return to the Realm of the Faeries as soon as the next opportunity was afforded to her.

# Chapter Twenty:

## The Journey Begins

**B**evyn headed the group of men excited to begin his very first adventure and Zindel followed closely behind. Zindel was deep in thought. He had a good group of valiant men, but that was all he had. What would happen when they came across a faerie or one of their many dangerous traps? He needed them to come together and actually become a team. He listened for a while. He heard nothing but the footsteps they were making. He had to get them talking, he had to get to know them, and get the group to know each other. Suddenly right then and there he heard laughter. He listened to whose laughter it was.

"Gwynn, would you care to share your laughter with all of us?"

Gwynn replied without laughter, in a most serious tone of voice.

"Razial and I were just discussing your wisdom and your

youthful appearance. Zindel, please tell Razial and myself your age."

Zindel was surprised. He never thought in all the situations possible that his men would be conversing amongst themselves about him.

"Why should it concern yourselves what my age is?"

Razial piped up.

"Come now Zindel, no man should be afraid of his own age. I will tell everyone, I am forty-six. I'll bet I'm the oldest as well, so now none of you should feel bad about it."

Gwynn decided to share his youthfulness.

"I am twenty-four, and extremely handsome for my age. Don't you all agree?"

Bevyn suddenly turned around and started walking backwards so that he too might be able to have his input.

"I'm sixteen!"

Zindel looked at this youthful little lad.

"Zindel, how long have you been a knight?"

Zindel had to recall that knowledge. It was almost too long ago to remember.

"I have been serving the King for fifteen years."

Bevyn's mouth dropped open.

"You do not look in your thirties."

Razial piped up once again.

"No he certainly does not."

Zindel suddenly saw a way to make his group of men into a team.

"I've got an idea to pass the time. You must say something about yourself and then guess my age. I will tell you if you are right or wrong."

Zindel waited in silence, would his men reject the idea? Would they find his age not worthy if they had to work for it? Suddenly the silence was broken, and Zindel was very much relieved.

"All right," Bevyn started, "I live with my ma and pa, and I am your squire Sir Zindel. I think you are twenty-nine."

Zindel laughed at the boy.

"I believe the idea was to say something nobody knew about you."

"Come now Zindel, you promised!"

Bevyn whined.

"Wrong my boy, but you flatter me much!"

Razial was the next to speak.

"About ten years ago, my house burnt down and I have been surviving at my mother and father's house as well. I believe they were very much obliged to my taking leave; How about thirty-one?"

Zindel had to look back at Razial. He did not think Razial would volunteer that information, but Zindel was too curious to let it pass.

"A fire you say? How did it start?"

Zindel questioned. Razial answered almost immediately.

"Ah Zindel, on my next turn perhaps, but for now you must answer as you've promised."

"Yes, yes Razial forgive me. You are of course incorrect."

Gwynn flung his hair into the wind, and started his fact about himself.

"I was born with light brown hair, but as I spent my days working in the fields, which may I add, is also how I got my rippling muscles, my hair turned to a wonderful golden blonde. I got my gorgeously blue eyes from both my Mother and Father. My Mother has a deep blue eye color while my father has a lighter blue eye color. Mixed you get this beautiful color. I have three loves in my life, my Mother, her cooking and myself. Are you twenty-nine?"

Bevyn nearly exploded at this comment.

"Gwynn I've already asked that age! Can you not listen to what other people are saying?!?"

Gwynn looked shocked. He turned to the rest of the men.

"Excuse me, but can someone tell me why this child is yelling at me?"

Razial commented in a much calmer tone.

"Gwynn if we are ever going to guess Zindel's age, we must work together."

Gwynn seemed to understand. Zindel commented on Gwynn's statement.

"So Gwynn, there is no lady love that could possibly be a wife someday?"

Gwynn suddenly had a disgusted face, though few of the men saw this.

"No woman is worthy of my beauty, nor could any of them handle it."

Razial's face took on the looks of shock and dismay at this comment.

"Gwynn, have you no heart? You think you can live without love. It's no life at all, believe you me."

Zindel was starting to understand something about Razial. His movements showed signs of fatiguing weariness brought on by the loss of his home, though he seemed to care deeply for anyone who would show him compassion of some kind. Gwynn on the other hand was something else. Very conceded, that was certainly noticeable. They continued to guess his age, only going up one year at a time. His young appearance was not wasted however. He learned a great deal about his men. Razial guessed once more.

"Zindel, you must be forty-seven."

Zindel shook his head and Razial's face dropped.

"You are pulling my leg Zindel. I myself am only forty-six and you appear years younger. What's your secret?"

Zindel stopped walking and turned to Razial.

"What's yours?"

Razial knew he must sacrifice another one of his many secrets.

"My wife and child were in the house when it burned down."

Zindel suddenly felt very sorry he had asked, even though he already knew. Everyone grew incredibly quiet.

"I am thirty-six. You skipped right over that one."

The plan, with the exception of Razial's final revelation, worked brilliantly. The group started to show signs of camaraderie that would hopefully sustain them through the many dark nights to come.

When King Xavier ordered them to leave at mid-day the men did not travel as far as Zindel imagined they would if they had started with a full day. As it was, they came to the edge of the Elvine Forest where a faerie named Jeanie was known to live. Zindel stopped his men for the night.

"Listen, the first faerie we will encounter is Jeanie and she lives in this forest."

Bevyn started to get excited.

"You mean there is a real Faerie in there? All this time they were never that far from home?!"

The group of men laughed. Zindel smiled at the innocence that shined through Bevyn's eyes at that very moment.

"Bevyn my boy, the Faeries are all around us."

Zindel returned his attention to the men.

"We will have the better advantage if we wait until morning to enter the Forest at all, so let us make camp here for the night."

The men separated out as they had done in the King's courtyard. They still had plenty of meat from their hunting lesson and their water pouches were full. The men fell asleep quite at their ease. Bevyn however stayed awake. He was waiting for an opportunity like this. He rolled over a little past midnight and without waking a soul drifted into the forest.

"I will show Zindel that I am more than capable to be on this quest."

Bevyn ventured farther into the forest, still talking to himself.

"I will talk to Jeanie and get the location of the Golden Staff of Enchantment out of her. Then Zindel will have kicked himself for ever asking to leave me behind."

Jeanie peered out from behind a tree. She had long blonde flowing hair, with huge green wings that were butterfly like. She giggled at Bevyn, he turned sharply toward the laugh, but Jeanie was already gone. She placed her hands to her mouth and made a small noise. Bevyn turned again and saw her. Jeanie started walking toward the boy very slowly. She was standing arms length away from him. Bevyn tried to speak but he forgot the meaning of his own words.

"Where is the Golden Staff of…the golden…you took it from Princess…I am with Sir…and we are here to find the…"

Bevyn was watching her hypnotic eyes. She looked directly into Bevyn's eyes. She gave him a playful smile and then she slowly turned and walked deeper into the forest. Bevyn followed the beautiful faerie and never even looked back.

# Chapter Twenty-One:

## The Elvine Forest

Zindel awoke the next morning and none of the other men were awake. Zindel was perplexed. All through the week, Bevyn had been awake before him and woken the other men. Zindel looked at where the little lad had fallen asleep the night before. He was not there. Zindel woke the other men.

"Have any of you seen Bevyn?!"

The men were sitting up, yawning, and wiping their eyes. Braen smiled to himself and Zindel saw it.

"Braen, have you seen Bevyn?"

Braen yawned again before answering him.

"Last night I saw him scamper off into the forest. I must have fallen asleep before he came back."

Zindel did not even have time to be angry with Braen for not waking him the moment he saw Bevyn wander off. He took off into the woods. The men dashed after him. Zindel was screaming Bevyn's name. He turned suddenly on the men that had followed him here.

"I need a quill pen!"

The men looked at him.

"SOMEBODY GET ME A QUILL PEN!"

The men started to check their pockets in a hurried fashion. Someone produced one though Zindel did not bother to look and see which pocket it had emerged. Zindel held the quill at arms length and spun around with it before letting it drop to the ground. As soon as the quill pen hit the ground, Jeanie flew from behind a tree. She stooped to pick up the assumed forgot quill pen and dash off again nobody the wiser, but Zindel knew it would happen. He grabbed her about her little faerie wrist just as her fingers were closing about the quill. Feeling very threatened and scared Jeanie tried to blend in with her surroundings, she was much like a chameleon in her ability to disappear. Most people would have let go in amazement or in frustration, but Zindel was wise to this as well. She reappeared with a sense of defeat. Zindel sat her down on a nearby tree stump.

"Jeanie I am Sir Zindel, a Knight from Wyveren," Zindel paused here and then shouted at her. "WHAT HAVE YOU DONE WITH BEVYN?!"

Jeanie turned her head and giggled at Zindel.

"We had fun last night! Not that he remembers it now. He is already gone."

Zindel squeezed her wrist tighter as he fought to hold himself together. He composed himself and began questioning her again.

"Jeanie, I am on a quest to seek the Golden Staff of Enchantment, which was stolen from Princess Mabli."

Jeanie sat silent as the trees twiddling her hair with her free hand and pretending not to be interested. Zindel snapped his fingers and another quill pen was produced to him. He dangled it just out of her reach.

"Speak Jeanie and you may have it forever."

Jeanie's eyes watched the quill pen dangle back and forth before she finally broke.

"I have heard of the Golden Staff of Enchantment, but I have it not. Perhaps you should try Tareedah in the Carolett Forest, for she may have more knowledge than I."

Zindel dropped the quill pen at her feet and called forth his men. Kyle watched Jeanie on the forest floor as she picked up the quill pen and then disappeared. He ran to the front to argue with Zindel.

"How do you know she is telling the truth?!"

Zindel answered without even turning his head to look at Kyle.

"All Faeries tell the truth, they cannot lie. If they do then they loose their immortality."

Kyle was silenced. The men followed Zindel keeping their true goal in mind. They must find Princess Mabli's Golden Staff of Enchantment. Her very life depended on it.

# Chapter Twenty-Two:

## The Sleeping Spell

The men came across an opening in the forest just as the sun was setting. Many of them carried wood in their arms. Zindel stopped in the middle of the clearing and started giving orders as to the proper construction of their camp.

"Kyle, Trent, Razial, head into the forest and hunt for dinner. Do not venture out of sight of one another. If you should happen to get lost, or come into any trouble shoot an arrow on fire straight up into the sky."

With that, the three men left, dropping their wood at their feet. Zindel turned to look at the others.

"Cole, Dagon, form a wood pile somewhere. Not too far away now, just a few footsteps away."

Cole and Dagon looked at each other. Both were dwarfed in size and would look very funny dragging pieces of wood that were far bigger than they were to a pile. They set off to their task. Not really acknowledging each other. Zindel turned once more to his men and glanced about the campsite.

"Morgan, gather some stones, big ones mind you, for a fire ring."

Morgan set off at once.

"Owen, Awstin, go in search of a river. We will need fresh water. Do not venture out of sight of one another. Take everyone's water pouch and fill it. When you get back let me know where the river resides."

Both men gathered water pouches from the men remaining at the camp and set off in the opposite direction as the hunters.

"Seith, Tristram, and Erwin, you three shall skin, gut, and cook the animals once they return to camp."

Zindel looked at the remaining three men left standing in front of him, waiting for orders. Zindel's eyes fell upon Kay.

"Kay, I want you to start the fire. It can take a while to really get it going. Start now and get the fire hot and ready to cook on."

Kay took off towards the woodpile. Zindel turned towards the last two men; Gwynn and Braen. He seemed to be out of tasks to do.

"Gwynn, Braen, check your bags for something to start the fire with."

Both men looked into their bags. It was hard to find something to spare really. They had salt and other sorts of faerie repellant charms. The truth was they did not know what they could do without.

"Zindel, I have some parchment here."

Gwynn finished looking through his bag first. Braen looked up and with drew an axe.

"This is about as useful as I can be Zindel."

Zindel looked at what he was given. He looked upward toward the darkening sky.

"That will work, hand me the parchment and the axe."

They handed their supplies over to Zindel who started to tear the parchment into tiny strips and placed them in the newly built fire ring. He then proceeded to take the axe and start scraping the blade on one of the rocks forming the fire ring. Then he started to swing the axe, full blown onto the rock. The men remaining in the campsite all stopped their assigned task for a moment and turned to look at Zindel. Was he going mad? Losing Bevyn was a terrible thing to happen, but to try to chop a rock. Zindel had favored Bevyn over all the other men. Perhaps it was because he was the first to volunteer, or because he was Zindel's squire, the other men did not know why exactly. Zindel however did know what he was doing. Soon small sparks started to fly from the rock and axe and land on the paper. Zindel kept on hacking. As soon as there were close to one hundred little orange sparks in the fire ring Zindel dropped to his hands and knees and gently began to blow on them. The men saw the sparks glow brighter with the wind. Kay grabbed a few good looking twigs and started to head toward the fire ring. Zindel was giving his third breath to the sparks when all of a sudden the parchment caught fire. Zindel jumped to his feet and Kay gently placed the kindling in the flames. Kay built up a beautiful fire, which all the remaining men sat around. As soon as the sunset Owen and Awstin came out into the clearing and started to pass around full water pouches.

"Were there any problems?"

Zindel asked. Owen and Awstin both shook their heads. They seemed to get along very well with each other. About a half an hour after Owen and Awstin came back there were footsteps from the other side of the clearing. Kyle, Trent, and Razial came out through the woods with rabbits draped around their necks. Seith, Tristram, and Erwin got up and went over to the men. They relieved them of their rabbits and went to work skinning, gutting, and then cooking them.

"Were there any problems?"

Trent seemed to be the only one to want to say anything.

"There was an abundance of rabbit I noticed."

Kyle suddenly jumped in.

"There was this great big deer and I had a perfect shot at him but…"

Razial cut him off.

"I told him that Zindel said to get enough to eat, and we already had the rabbit."

Once the men had eaten and had their fill of water from their pouches, their conversation drifted from various things to other various things. It finally landed on one topic that tugged on Zindel's heartstrings, Bevyn. Zindel could hardly hold his head proudly. Now his men were aware of how far the faeries would go, but at Bevyn's expense. He should have not let Bevyn go with them.

"Bevyn couldn't have been much help to us really. He was only a boy, without much knowledge of what he was doing. Yet that is the sad part, his life had barely begun."

The men all nodded together. At one point during the silence, they all had the same thoughts about Bevyn. He was so young, what was Zindel thinking allowing him to come. Nobody dared to speak this last part aloud because they all knew of Zindel's affection for the boy. Zindel continued to speak.

"Even though I didn't know Bevyn that long, he seemed so close to me, like he was a son."

"Ever father any children Zindel?"

Razial asked quietly. Zindel was caught off guard.

"I suppose I did."

"You suppose you did? How can you suppose you fathered children? You either did or you didn't."

Gwynn protested. There was a sharp slap heard from the other side of the fire, followed by the whining of Gwynn. Owen's voice was heard sharply speaking to Gwynn.

"Are you the town loon?! Never, ever question that to a man. He could have personal problems, ever think of that?"

Zindel stood to see them better over the blazing fire.

"Owen, there is no need for that…"

"Owen! I had my hair perfect and you ruined it!"

Gwynn interrupted.

"Well it serves you right for asking such a stupid question."

Owen shot back. Zindel tried to speak again.

"Owen, Gwynn."

Both stopped and looked at Zindel.

"Right, yes I have fathered a few children…three. No problems Owen, I just…lost them. I--had two daughters and…but they are gone now."

The men eyed Zindel, accepted what he had said and they all sat gazing into the blazing fire once more. They were all silent, something Gwynn was unaccustomed to. He started to look around the campsite. He saw a purplish-bluish glow arising from somewhere in the woods. Gwynn elbowed Kyle.

"What do you suppose that is?"

Kyle looked beyond Gwynn and stared at the glow,

mesmerized. Zindel caught their glare and also saw the glow. One by one, they all started to stare. Kyle grabbed an axe and slowly stood. Zindel stood sharply and motioned for Kyle to put the axe down. Zindel made a motion for Kyle and all the men to stay where they were while he went over toward the glow. When he peered over the bush where the glow was emitting from he sighed and motioned for his men to join him. They hurried and peered over the bush to see a teenage girl asleep. Zindel suddenly broke the silence with a whisper, which startled most of the men.

"She is the Sleeping Vulnerability, or as she is more commonly known, Lucille. She appears as a young soul, always asleep. She creates vulnerability wherever she goes. Mostly she appears when women lose their children or loved ones. She becomes a thing of power, that helps them accept what has happened, and move on to have more children, or to love again. She must be here because we lost Bevyn."

Kyle reached out a hand to touch her. He had always wanted to touch a faerie, but they were all so fast. He was almost at her cheek when Zindel's hand flew out of nowhere and clamped hard around Kyle's wrist.

"Never touch her. The consequences would be most horrible. She is the virginal maiden of all the faeries, and they would not stop until you die a most terrible death, should something happen to her during her eternal sleep."

Zindel released Kyle's wrist and gave him a most piercing glare. Kyle ran his hand over his wrist where Zindel had grabbed so suddenly.

"How is it, that you know all there is to know about each faerie?"

Kyle directed toward Zindel. Zindel stopped to think for a minute.

"King Xavier and Princess Mabli have always been obsessed with the Faeries. It would be impossible to work for the King and not know something about them."

The men were still gazing at the sleeping faerie. Even Gwynn was staring. Owen teased him.

"What's the matter Gwynn? Is she more beautiful than you?"

Gwynn made a face at him.

"No creature is more beautiful than I Owen. Don't be silly."

With that said Gwynn retreated to the fire. Owen followed him and one by one all the men went back to the fire. This just left Zindel and Kyle.

"I meant what I said Kyle. Don't touch her, don't even breathe on her."

Zindel walked away, watching Kyle. He too got up and walked back to the fire. The men settled down for the night and Kyle fell asleep facing the glow of the sleeping faerie. When the moon was high in the sky and the fire was nothing but glowing coals Kyle awoke facing the glow in the woods. He glanced around and saw that all the others were sleeping. He quietly stood and tiptoed over to the sleeping faerie. He peered over the bushes that hid her.

"What could one touch do?"

He bent over and slowly outstretched his hand. He closed his eyes, thinking if anything should happen that would protect him. He touched her face and noticed that her creamy white skin was silky smooth and her blonde curly hair was like velvet. He started to stroke her hair and he slowly opened his eyes and glared at her lovingly. He jumped into the bushes and lay next to her and he kissed her; one simple kiss on the lips and he fell asleep. When he awoke again she was gone, the sun was just beginning to rise. He hurried back to where he fell asleep the night before, and pretended to be asleep once more.

# Chapter Twenty-Three:

## The Keeper of Memories

I t seemed it was half an hour before any of the other men even stirred. Kyle tried to get back to sleep, but found he was unable. Not from lack of trying however. He felt tired. How long had he stayed awake with Lucille? He seemed positively drained of energy, though he thought he had slept some of the time that he was with her. As he was thinking about the length of sleep he got, Zindel stirred. Kyle rolled over and pretended to just be waking. Zindel looked in his direction, and then over to where Lucille's glow was the previous evening.

"Kyle, walk with me to the river. You look like you could do with some fresh water."

Kyle nodded, thinking he was safe. Zindel would have noticed him returning had he been awake. Zindel reached the water first and knelt down to splash some water on his face. Kyle knelt down also to follow Zindel. He placed his hands in the water, brought the cool water to his face, and immersed his face in it. The moment this happened Kyle felt more tired than ever. He closed his eyes as though he was attempting to fall asleep at that moment. His eyes snapped right back open. Zindel was watching him.

"Kyle did you not sleep very well last night? You look like you could sleep kneeling where you are right now."

Kyle looked at Zindel and thought for a moment.

"Sleeping on the ground is quite an adjustment. I'll bet none of the other's slept like they would at home."

Zindel continued to stare at him. Something was off.

"You didn't try to lull yourself to sleep over by Lucille did you?"

Kyle's face gave away the answer before he could even try to hide it. Zindel was outraged.

"Kyle! What did I tell you?! Now they are not going to let you sleep undisturbed."

Kyle was confused.

"Who isn't going to let me sleep undisturbed?"

"The faeries aren't going to, any of them. I told you something terrible would happen to you if anything happened to her!"

Kyle was relieved.

"So what, I've been without sleep before. No big deal. Wow, you really had me worried with all that die a most terrible death speech."

Zindel stared blankly at Kyle.

"How long have you ever been without sleep Kyle?"

Kyle scratched his head while thinking about it.

"Oh I don't know. Trent and I had a contest once and both of us were awake for about two and a half days straight."

Zindel laughed to himself.

"This is a good punishment. I must admit."

"What do you mean?"

"I imagine the faeries will keep you awake until you die."

Kyle stared at Zindel.

"I feel fine Zindel."

They walked back to camp. Most of the men had risen. Only Gwynn was still asleep. The men paused to look at Zindel and Kyle.

"Someone wake up Gwynn, it's time to move out."

Owen smiled and went to get a full pouch of ice-cold river water. The men traveled through the rest of the forest. They spent all morning walking through a plain field. They came to a river mid day. They all stopped to rest and refill their water pouches. Kyle looked at himself in the water reflection. He looked fine. Zindel must have been wrong. He could not wait until they stopped for nightfall though. He was tired and walking all day was a draining activity. Zindel called them onward. The sun was beating against their backs. Every bit of shade they came across they used. Zindel was getting quite upset with the frequent stopping. Razial was wiping the sweat from his brow when he looked up and saw what looked like a forest looming in the distance.

"Zindel, what forest is that?"

Zindel turned and smiled.

"That, my friend, is our destination. Alright men, listen up."

All the men turned toward Zindel to listen.

"We are approaching the Carolett Forest. We all remember what happened to young Bevyn. It can just as easily happen with Tareedah. She is the faerie of the dusk, and the keeper of all memories. Think of nothing while passing through here;

for if Tareedah senses your weaknesses, she will use them against you."

Razial was silent. He had thought of nothing else this trip than his dear wife and daughter. How could he possibly put something like that out of his mind? He decided that Zindel's warning was simply an over reaction because of Bevyn. He knew his wife and daughter were dead. What could Tareedah use on him? They entered the Carolett forest by minutes before the sunset. Zindel stepped cautiously awaiting for twilight to set in; for that was the only time of day Tareedah could be seen. Zindel suddenly spotted her at the riverbank, watching the water. She was a faerie with sparkles that look like diamonds on her eyelashes. She had small blue wings with dazzling spots in them. Her hair was short, chestnut brown and curly. Zindel had to lure her to him. He closed his own eyes and thought hard about his own dear hometown, and how he was exiled from his loving wife and children. He thought of how much he loved them and how much he missed them. It was working; Tareedah slowly turned her head and looked directly at Zindel. She slowly started to ascend toward the men. Zindel kept thinking and Tareedah was right in front of Zindel. She had transformed into Zindel's wife. He was the only one who could see his wife standing before him. All the other men saw the petite faerie. She hugged him and went to kiss him on the lips, just the way his wife would have. However, he grabbed a hold of her arms and immediately she was Tareedah again in Zindel's eyes. He held her at arms length.

"Tareedah, I am Sir Zindel, a knight from Wyveren."

Tareedah was fighting her hardest to get out of his grip, but Zindel was stronger.

"I am on a quest to find the Golden Staff of Enchantment

which was stolen from Princess Mabli. Tareedah, I need to know who took it."

She fought to get away. She was starting to panic. Zindel thought again of his wife and Tareedah transformed before his eyes. She softened into Zindel and rested her head on his shoulder. She closed her eyes and breathed the scent of him in.

"Tareedah, tell me who has it."

Tareedah looked longingly at him, and then she spoke calmly.

"I know not who has it. However I do not doubt that it is Velelia or Mouyra."

Zindel released her, but she did not fly away. She continued to stand in Zindel's arms. She looked lovingly at him and went to touch his hair when she stopped and starred at one of the men. Her entire demeanor changed and Zindel noticed this. She was starring at Erwin. She had the same loving expression in her eyes and Zindel quickly walked passed her to draw attention away from Erwin. She stood shocked and angry as she watched his men follow him, each of them turning a blind eye to her. When they were all out of hearing range, she spoke to herself.

"If he will not give into me, then I will make him pay!"

She then flew after them. Razial was trotting behind the men to keep up with them.

"Now, there was nothing wrong with thinking of my wife and daughter through here. Nothing happened."

He suddenly heard a child's laughter as he finished his thought. He looked around, but saw nothing. He realized he was falling further behind the group. He ran to catch up, but a child and her mother ran out in front of him. The child stopped and looked at Razial and so did the mother.

They both started to run toward him. The child reached him first.

"Daddy oh how I've missed you!"

Razial started to cry. Could it be that his own little daughter was hugging him? He felt her around him; he felt her hair and her face. She was really there. He picked her up and hugged her. He spun her around and kissed her on the forehead. Then he looked up at his wife. Her eyes were glowing as they always were. He hugged her too. He smelled her hair and kissed her face.

"Razial, you don't know how we've missed you!"

Razial stopped. He was being foolish. His wife and daughter were dead and this was all Tareedahs doing. He had to stop thinking of them, for Zindel was right. Tareedah was trying to lure him to her world to never return; but how was it that they were standing here in front of him? They were not hallucinations; you could not hug and kiss hallucinations.

"Where have you been since the fire?"

Razial questioned them. His wife lovingly slipped her hand into his.

"Razial we were not in the house when the fire started. We went for a walk in the woods. We got so lost, and have not been able to find home. I knew you would come looking for us, so we stayed in this little area."

Razial could not believe it.

"I know it is you Tareedah. My wife and child are dead and gone. Thank you for the lovely reunion, but I will not be going with you."

Tareedah changed in front of Razial's eyes.

"Tell me Razial, have you ever heard of a Changeling?"

Razial stood still. Amazed at the faerie standing where his wife and daughter just were. He stuttered slightly.

"Uh…Ch…Changelings? They are switched with human babies before they are baptized."

"Correct you are. Now tell me, were you aware that your own little daughter was one?"

Razial stared directly at her for a moment.

"You are telling falsehoods!"

Tareedah smiled.

"Now, now Razial think back. Your daughter was born on a seventh year. Every seven years the faeries will take many human babies and leave behind changelings. With our magic, you never know the difference. Usually the changeling dies, but a very few of them survive. Before the fire were you not talking with your wife about how queer your own little daughter was acting recently?"

Razial thought back.

"She was saying strange things in a voice that was not her own. She said I have seen the egg before the hen. I have seen the first acorn before the oak. But I have never seen brewing in an eggshell before."

Tareedah gave a little chuckle.

"And you went out to get a doctor. However, your wife knew better. She threw the changeling into the fire and it flew up and away out the chimney. And your little daughter was supposed to appear at the front door."

Razial got mad.

"That is the deal is it not. If the parents find out and dispose of the changeling they get their own child back!"

"Not one so valuable to us. The child appeared and we were soon to follow. We took your wife and daughter and burned down your house."

Razial grabbed his hair and started to cry.

"You lie! None of this is true. My wife and daughter are dead!"

Tareedah took his hand.

"I can take you to them."

He looked up at her. She had sincerity in her eyes.

"Come Razial; let me take you to your family."

Tareedah led him deep into the forest. Zindel stopped the group and looked back. His heart ached, yet he knew not why. Perhaps it was all this thinking of his wife and children. Something was missing, something was not right.

"Where is Razial?"

Owen looked behind him.

"Well he was trailing behind me; but he is older so I'll bet we were a little fast for him. We better stop and wait."

They did stop and wait, but it was not long before Zindel went through the crowd of men.

"I will be back, set up camp here for the night."

Zindel dashed back the way he came. Tareedah flew blindly into his path.

"What is the hurry Zindel?"

He stopped for he was a bit breathless.

"Where is Razial?"

Tareedah did not answer. Instead, she went to kiss Zindel. He refused her again.

"Zindel why are you so cold to me? Why can't it be as it once was?"

Zindel looked at her.

"Tareedah, what it once was, got me banished from the realm of the faeries. I lost my immortality for my deceitful lies to Tessah."

Tareedah looked into Zindel's eyes.

"I took Razial to his family. He is happier than he has ever been. Leave him be Zindel."

Zindel could have kicked himself. Tareedah glanced behind Zindel and saw that Erwin had appeared, he had been listening the entire time. Zindel's face took on a look of shock and dismay. He took a few more steps forward.

"Zindel, you are a…one of them?"

Tareedah smiled at him with a certain kind of fondness. Zindel looked from Erwin to her.

"You are his mother?"

Tareedah glanced at Zindel for a moment before turning back to her son.

"My son, I have missed you!"

Tears welled up in her eyes as she held her arms out and Erwin went to them without hesitation. Tareedah attempted to pull Zindel into the hug as well but he stepped out of reach.

"Honestly Zindel, I can understand that you do not want to hug me, but your own son?"

Zindel's eyes widened now and Erwin looked at him. Together they spoke.

"He is my…but how?"

Tareedah laughed.

"I think you remember how Zindel. Erwin my dear he was exiled before your birth—even before he knew of your conception. I desperately wanted to keep you—but we have rules about boys. You were taken from my arms the moment you were born. I had hopes of keeping you, for if Queen Tessah had another girl than you would have been the rightful heir to the throne."

Zindel now found his voice.

"Then Tessah had a boy?! I have a son...I have two sons?"

Tareedah smiled evilly.

"Oops, I have said too much already."

Tareedah disappeared. Zindel looked at Erwin.

Erwin stuttered for a moment.

"I...I know that you did not know about me Zindel. And even if you had known you were exiled; But why could my mother not keep me?"

Zindel sighed.

"Long ago Erwin, before my time, the Faeries were allowed to keep boys, but boys didn't respond well to the magic. They become mad and murderous. Only girls are safe."

Erwin was quiet for another second.

"You were a Faerie though...you were King. I am full faerie by birth. I would not have been affected. They—she could have kept me."

Zindel shook his head again.

"There was a prophecy made long ago, after the Goodwin-Fernandez war, that states two sons born of the same father will destroy the world as we know it. So the Ancestral Order made it so no King would ever have more than one son."

Erwin was starring at his leader in shock.

"I am living proof that they failed."

Zindel tried to explain to his son.

"No, you are proof that I failed. A King is supposed to stay faithful to his queen. Until the child is born and takes, his first breath the King remains fertile. Tessah was pregnant—very pregnant when the affair happened."

Erwin felt worse now than he had all his life growing up and knowing that the people he called family had taken him out of duty. He loved them and they loved him, but he was not theirs, he did not belong to them and now he knew why. He was not half-human—half-faerie, he was full faerie, and he had been banished from the life he was meant to have because someone else had a boy first.

"I am of Royal blood Zindel, your royal blood. I belong in the Realm of the Faeries. I should not be punished for your crimes."

Zindel was trying to remain calm.

"Erwin, what do you want from me? I have no power, no say what happens here. I was stripped of my wings just as you were. There is nothing I can do to get you or me into their world again."

"OUR WORLD, Zindel. It is yours and mine. We belong there. Not here…not here."

Zindel thought for a while.

"When I was banished, they were starting experiments on turning humans into Faeries. Perhaps when we reach someone who has the power to do something, we can talk."

Erwin's face spread into a smile.

"Zindel, I am so happy. I will finally belong somewhere I am suppose to belong."

Zindel turned his head away from Erwin before he spoke again.

"There is one condition Erwin."

Erwin was still smiling.

"Anything you say…Father."

Zindel faltered here. He had never known the outcome of Tessah's third child. This was the first time he had ever heard his son's voice recognize him. He quickly recovered his composer.

"You will never be in-line for the Throne. If the Ancestral

Order agrees to turn us, or you, back into faeries you will not be of legitimate birth to become King."

Erwin kept on smiling.

"I do not care about becoming King. Just being with people like me, will be enough."

Zindel smiled finally and placed one hand on his shoulder.

"Then I must ask you one more thing…son."

Erwin beamed at this title.

"Anything."

"Please do not share anything you have learned today with the other men. I do not believe they would follow me if they knew the truth."

They returned to the other to tell them that they had lost Razial.

# Chapter Twenty-Four:

## Lodstreuo

Zindel awoke the next morning. He sat up slowly and looked around at his sleeping men. His eyes starred fondly at his son for a moment before moving on. Then they fell on Kyle, who was sitting straight up and looking blankly out into the forest. Zindel walked over to him.

"Did you sleep at all last night Kyle?"

Kyle looked sharply toward Zindel's voice because he had not heard him come up behind him.

"Yea I slept on and off."

His answer was short and Zindel had a sudden suspicion that Kyle had not slept at all.

Zindel and his men continued through the Carolett Forest. Zindel could not understand it. He was losing men like crazy. Had he not warned them enough? Could they not learn from Bevyn? Zindel was so lost in his own thoughts he stepped right off the level ground and started to fall down a steep lowering hill that leveled out into a huge mud pit. Just as he was about to fall face first into the pit he was pulled back by the collar of his shirt. When Zindel had stabilized himself, he looked up to see Awstin.

"Thank you Awstin."

Awstin nodded. Zindel looked out at the smooth mud lake. He looked left and right. He continued to talk.

"We must pass through this mud. Unfortunately, there is no other way around it. This is a defense mechanism of the Faeries, a moat."

The men could sense the tone in Zindel's voice. It was full of anxiety and fear. They started to get excited, because they were yet to see a fight. Most of the men were beginning to wonder why Zindel had equipped them with weapons in the first place.

"Okay, follow me in a line through the mud; one man behind the other. No one is to step out of line."

Zindel descended into the mud, waste deep holding his sword above his head. Most of the men followed in the same fashion. Owen was holding his sword with one hand over his shoulder when about half way through the mud Owen remembered that morning how Gwynn, who had been sleeping next to him, kept complaining of a smell and not very discreetly sniffing in his direction. Owen took a whiff of the mud and delighted in its stagnant, putrid odor. Owen took his free hand, scooped up a mud ball, and sent it flying directly at Gwynn.

"OWEN!!!"

Was the cry heard from the back, apparently it was a direct hit. Owen, who tried to hide his delight was whistling and looking around innocently, turned toward Gwynn.

"Yes?"

Gwynn hurtled a mud ball back at him, but he ducked and the ball hit Awstin in the back of the head. Awstin turned slowly and saw Owen doubled over with laughter and immediately scooped up a mud ball and aimed for him. He swerved just in time and the mud splattered all over Kyle. Kyle fell forward in the mud and was completely covered on the front side of his body. When he stood up again, the entire group of men had stopped and everyone but Owen was covered in mud. They ganged up on him and dunked him under. Zindel this whole time was standing on the shore yelling at the men to stop this madness and get out of the mud. The men were having far too much fun however and this cry fell onto deaf ears. Owen came up from being under the mud and went to push the first person he could find when he was suddenly pulled back under. Whatever had him had claws, and the more he struggled the tighter its grip got. Owen kicked with his free leg in hopes of hitting its eye, or breaking its nose or jaw. The men above were throwing mud at each other, completely oblivious to a missing fellow. Only Zindel noticed Owen's disappearance. His voice finally rang out through the mud fight.

"Where is Owen?!"

The men stopped fighting and started to look around at each other. Then suddenly Trent was pulled right into the mud as well. Several men went right after him. They got a hold of his hand and slowly started to pull him back. As soon as Trent's head was above the mud, he started yelling.

"It's got claws! It's pulling me down!"

Suddenly something grabbed Gwynn's ankle and he screamed. The men who were not helping with Trent went to help Gwynn.

"It's got my ankle it's got my ankle!"

However, they noticed that Gwynn was not being sucked underneath. Kyle went down and pulled up a hand.

"It's Owen! Pull him up!"

The men rescued Owen from the mud and quickly revived him to normal standing abilities. Now all the men went to pull the rest of Trent out of the mud. When they got him, a huge pile of mud came up too. The monstrous mud pile suddenly had an eye and a mouth. When it opened its mouth, a bunch of little tongues came out and each tongue was the size of one man complete with its own mouth and a set of razor sharp teeth. The men all drew their swords prepared to fight this thing or die trying. Suddenly Zindel was with his men. He had run back through the mud to be with them.

"Cut off the tongues! Blind it!"

The men catapulted Dagon up to the monster's eye, sword first. It was a miss; the sword landed right where the nose would be if it had one. It screamed when that happened. The men could not stand the cry of the thing. Many covered their ears. Dagon tried to pull the sword out of the monster and try again but one of the tongues caught him around the middle. It wrapped him like a boa constrictor would wrap its prey and the tongue sunk its razor sharp teeth into him. Owen thinking fast brought down his sword hard on the body of the monster that he could reach. It screamed again but it did not release Dagon from its deadly grip. Dagon was starting to become weak; his hand was slipping from his grip on his sword. Zindel brought his sword above his head and started to charge at the monster. He was not going to lose another man over this. The men all followed Zindel together.

"Attack together!"

The men all started to chop the mud monster's body.

The remaining tongues came down to wrap them all. One wrapped itself around Owen's arm. He took his sword with one hand raised above his head and brought it down, slicing the tongue in half. The monster screamed so piercingly, but released Dagon. Dagon sat for a moment on the monsters face catching his breath. Zindel cried at him while cutting a tongue free of his leg.

"Dagon, blind the monster, now!"

Dagon stood up and pulled his sword out of the monster's face. He brought the sword above his head, blade facing downward and jammed it directly into the monster's big red eye. Suddenly the mud fell beneath Dagon. It was as if the monster disappeared completely. One of the tongues, however, grabbed hold of Dagon's middle upon his fall. He fell directly into the mud and was pulled under in one swift motion. Someone grabbed his wrist. He was forcefully being pulled back to the surface. As soon as the tongue was revealed, it was cut. Dagon stood and smiled at Zindel, who had pulled him up and at Awstin who had cut the tongue. Zindel led them out of the mud and they stood on the bank of the mud hole. Kyle collapsed on the bank to rest. They were all reliving their triumph. Zindel was not looking pleased.

"Next time I tell you not to step out of line, I expect you to listen! We could have lost more than time out there!"

Awstin was laughing.

"Come now Zindel, we defeated the monster!"

Zindel drew a step closer to him.

"It was luck. What if there had been two? I am trying to keep you out of danger, so that we might finish our quest and return home safely."

Owen countered Zindel.

"Well Zindel, we did work together to defeat him."

Zindel glared at Owen. He slowly and cautiously back away. Zindel started turning this over in his head. The boy was right. He did not know how to listen, but he was right about this. For the first time, this entire quest all the men pulled together and worked as what they were a team. Zindel continued to glare at Owen. He could not forget that he had started this whole mess.

"I suppose you are right Owen. You all have done exactly what I have been wanting."

Zindel forced a smile then started to walk.

"Come, there is a river down here with fresh water. Let us bathe the filth away."

The men followed him. Owen watched Gwynn try to pull mud out of his hair.

"The mud isn't the only reason Zindel wants you to bathe Gwynn," Owen sniffed him. "What is that awful smell? It is horrible."

Gwynn turned around to look at him.

"You know, Owen, mud is actually very good for the skin."

Gwynn threw a handful of mud and hit Owen directly in the face. Owen chuckled to himself, scraped it off, and followed everyone else down to the river.

# Chapter Twenty-Five:

## Braen's Obsession

The men had cleaned themselves the best they could. Zindel told the tail of what it was exactly that they fought that night around the campfire.

"That was not a monster made of mud. It was the species called Lodstreuo, an ancient faerie experiment gone wrong. Lodstreuo was derived from the leech; it was a normal leech, given faerie powers and magic. However instead of changing its diet as intended, the faeries only succeeded in growing it larger."

Awstin cocked his head.

"Why did they do this?"

Zindel smiled to himself.

"There is a pesky little bug back in Wyveren, it comes out at night."

Awstin nodded and Zindel continued.

"There are none here in the Realm of the Faeries. Lodstreuo

failed, but they found another way to rid the bug of their kingdom."

Braen seemed to like this idea.

"So the faeries, that did this, corrupted nature?"

Zindel thought for a second. He did not want to give the men bad ideas about the faeries. After all, not all of them were evil.

"No Braen. It is believed that Velelia got in the way of their experiment. She tampered with it and caused it to go incredibly wrong."

Braen seemed more interested than he had the entire quest.

"Who is Velelia?"

Zindel was suddenly uneasy about Braen's interest, but he still told her history.

"Velelia is also known as the Royal Ruthless Witch. She is actually not a faerie, but a queen of old who was obsessed with magic. Some say that she was born a witch and that is how she came to be queen in the first place. Other's say she made her court magician teach her. Once her peasants realized she was a witch they captured and tried to hang her. When they found that she had cast a spell to make herself invulnerable to being hanged they set fire to her. It is because of this reason that Velelia is intolerant of humans and will cast spells on those who cross her path. She mainly turns them into forest animals."

Cole shuddered at that explanation.

"I like living in the woodland, but to be a creature of it?"

Braen argued back.

"But Cole, don't you find it fascinating?"

Kay fired up at him.

"You find heathen magic fascinating? Why son, I'll bet she would turn you into the worst animal imaginable."

Zindel cut into the conversation.

"She turns you into the favorite prey of the animal you fear the most, then she transports you right in the middle of their habitat."

Braen's eyes lit up.

"That is genius!"

Zindel could do nothing but look at Braen, his words failed him. Gwynn just came into the conversation.

"So, if she is a witch, then she must be really ugly."

Braen got very defensive.

"No, I'll bet she is beautiful."

Kay and Cole looked at each other. Gwynn spoke again.

"Well, I suppose she could be a beautiful witch, but she won't be as pretty as me."

Gwynn said this as the wind blew through his hair. Braen scowled at him.

"It is no wonder you can't love anybody else Gwynn, you only have enough love for yourself."

Gwynn went into an outrage.

"I love my mother! And her cooking!"

Kay exploded on them both.

"Listen, both of you all this jabbering needs to stop. We have a very serious quest at hand. Princess Mabli is depending on us to find her Golden Staff."

Braen and Gwynn became hushed. Cole became curious.

"Zindel, what is the Golden Staff?"

Zindel had been waiting for this question, but he was reluctant to answer it.

"King Xavier assures me, it is of dire importance to Princess Mabli's health. That it holds magical, healing powers."

Cole snickered. Zindel questioned.

"What is so funny Cole?"

"Well Zindel, we don't need to go on this quest for that. The King could have called me. I have great herbal remedies."

Kay bellowed with laughter.

"And I have a drink that will get her moving in no time!"

Zindel was awed at the idea that a royal lady would drink anything that Kay had to offer. Or that the King would approve of herbal remedies.

"Well my lads, the King also expressed to me that if a faerie did get a hold of it and he or she used it to get some of our magic, they could easily take over the species."

Gwynn contributed.

"So, we are not really here to save Princess Mabli, but the human race?"

Zindel was shocked at the outlook Gwynn had.

"Yes, I suppose we are."

Braen piped up.

"So, what shall we do with the faerie that took the Golden Staff?"

Zindel had not really thought about this yet.

"Well, if it is a good faerie, who only took it for lust, then they will confess and return it."

Braen continued to push.

"And if it was an evil faerie?"

Zindel hesitated.

"Then we shall have to kill her."

Braen was silenced, while Owen who had been silent and listening until now, decided to join the conversation.

"Isn't there some kind of Chain of Command we will have to follow before we just execute one of their people?"

Zindel smiled at his interest.

"Oh yes. There is the Ancestral Order and of course a faerie King, or at least there was."

Owen was curious.

"Was?"

"Well, a long time ago, the Faerie King was married to Tessah, the current Faerie Queen. Well the King was found being intimate with another faerie; which happens to be an unspeakable crime in the realm of the faeries. So he was thrown out."

Owen was very interested.

"So there could be some guy out there, who might be four hundred years old and he only looks about thirty?"

Zindel laughed.

"No. You see the King lied about his intimacy, so he lost his immortality."

Braen came back into the conversation again.

"So does that make him an evil faerie?"

Zindel was extremely concerned with Braen's attraction to knowledge about the evil faeries.

"No Braen that makes him a mortal; a human man."

Gwynn came in again as well.

"Was he a handsome faerie?"

Zindel did not know how to answer this.

"I'd like to think he was."

Gwynn smiled.

"Good thing. All the faeries we have seen so far aren't exactly on the pretty side."

Zindel was upset with this comment. However, it was Kyle who spoke.

"All the faeries are pretty Gwynn, did you not see Lucille?"

Zindel shot a glare at Kyle. Kyle actually glared back at Zindel. Gwynn was completely oblivious to the stare down going on in front of him.

"Yes, I saw her. She was practically a child. How can a child be beautiful? Children are annoying and smelly."

Kyle stood up slowly and tried to draw his sword, but he could not pull it out far enough from the holster it sat in.

"No Gwynn, you are the one who is annoying and smelly."

Zindel stepped in, eyeing Kyle queerly.

"Well actually Gwynn, Lucille is the epitome of beauty to all faerie children."

Braen countered.

"Does that mean that evil faeries are ugly Zindel?"

Zindel thought about this.

"Not necessarily. In fact they may be more beautiful to lure men into doing things for them."

Braen smiled to himself and Kay directed a comment toward Braen.

"It does not matter how beautiful she is. If she has the Golden Staff, we kill her."

Zindel looked around at all his men.

"Let us call it a night men, that fight today really diminished my energy."

Everybody silently agreed and all settled into the dirt for some much needed rest. Kyle lay wide-awake on the ground looking up at the stars.

# Chapter Twenty-Six:

## Mabli's Secret

P rincess Mabli drifted into the room where her father sat. She was in a dreamy sort of state. King Xavier started when he saw her.

"Mabli you are alright!"

Mabli took a seat nearest to the King.

"Yes Father?"

King Xavier dismissed his servants before continuing his conversation with his daughter.

"I thought Stocking had kidnapped you!"

Mabli smiled at him.

"No Father. I escaped to somewhere safe where Stocking would not be able to find me. However, I failed to leave you a message of some kind of my well-being. So I came back to let you know that I was safe and that you need not worry about my absence." Mabli sighed and glanced out a window closest to her. "Today I feel absolutely wonderful! Today is such a beautiful day Father I feel that this day was made just for me!"

The King stared at his daughter silently.

"Father, I would like to ride the horses today."

The King took a sip from his cup finally breaking his piercing stare.

"I forbid it."

Mabli's face fell.

"Why do you forbid it?"

"Mabli, it is not safe for you outside the palace walls. Besides, I know you will ride to the forest."

Her face took on a look of surprise. The King continued to speak.

"The forest is a dangerous place. I can't have you playing there."

Mabli smiled again at her father.

"Well then, may I go swimming in the lake?"

King Xavier once again stared at his daughter. He looked her up and down.

"No."

Mabli became upset this time.

"Why Father? The lake is on the grounds inside the outer palace walls even. You have kept me inside the castle walls for more than a fortnight!"

"Don't think I don't know what you are doing in the forest, or rather who you are meeting Mabli."

Mabli's face was so stunned she could not have hid the truth if she tried.

"Mabli I forbid it! You will not go prancing around with that Faerie! I should have stopped this obsession with faeries when your Mother died I see what a mistake I've made."

Mabli's eyes were filled with tears.

"Mother loved them so much, Father you can't keep me from them I feel so close to Mother when I am with them."

King Xavier diverted his eyes.

"Stop this foolish crying. Tears are not going to bring your mother back and neither is prancing around with faeries!"

Mabli straightened herself up and looked her Father in the eye.

"This is the last link I have to Mother. You can not take it from me."

The King exploded at her.

"YOU ARE GOING TO TELL ME WHAT I CAN AND CAN NOT DO!?!?!"

Mabli immediately started to shake her head and look down at the floor.

"No, no Father."

The King relaxed and his face started to return to its flushed color. Mabli almost whispered her next sentence.

"But, Father, I must see them again."

The King picked up his goblet. He took a sip from it before looking at his daughter.

"Why?"

Mabli eased slightly in her chair.

"I must see them again to say good bye."

The King began to pick food off his plate again.

"That is nonsense Mabli. If I let you go say, good-bye you will never return to me. It is bad enough I have to let some other king's son run my kingdom. My daughter will be queen of this palace!"

Mabli stood from her chair, trying to hide her guilt.

"What makes you think I would run away?"

King Xavier stood with surprising ease to speak to his daughter's face.

"It is because you love him Mabli! I don't know who it is, but you are in love with one of them!"

Mabli stared her Father in the face and smiled at him.

"Yes Father, I am in love with one of them."

The King fell back into his throne. He finally said what he had been suspecting and his daughter did not even deny it. He sat silent in his throne for some time. Mabli stared at him, after a while, she actually kneeled at his feet. He finally spoke.

"Who is he?"

Mabli remained quiet.

"Tell me who he is Mabli!"

She looked at him.

"I will not. You would have him killed."

The King smiled and tried to play the fool.

"Why would I do such a thing to the...man...my daughter loves?"

Mabli stood up, looked down upon her Father, and finally exploded on him.

"I will tell you why Father, because you would die before letting a Faerie become king of your kingdom!"

The King stood once again and bellowed at the top of his voice.

"You are right at that! You cannot marry a faerie anyway you stupid girl. You are a Princess so you must marry a Prince!"

Mabli blurted the next part out without thinking.

"He is a Prince! He is Prince of the Faeries and he wants me to be his Princess and together we will be King and Queen in the realm of the faeries!"

The King watched his daughter as she smiled at the thought. She started to spin and laugh. Clearly, she had gone mad. Once she stopped and looked at her Father, he pointed his finger at her.

"They have corrupted you girl! You are not a faerie, you are a human!"

Upon finishing this sentence, King Xavier examined his daughter more closely. She had sparkles on her eyelashes and her skin seemed to have a handsome glow. He noticed that her robe was very tight about her throat.

"What have they done to you?!"

Mabli grabbed at the throat of her robe.

"They have done nothing to me."

Mabli started to run for the door but the King grabbed her by the back of her robe and tore it free from Mabli's grasp. Two faerie wings were starting to emerge from Mabli's back. Mabli turned to face her father in an attempt to hide the wings from him. There on a chain of metal Xavier had never seen before was the pendent that belonged to the Royal Family. Xavier tried to yank it off, but he only succeeded in throwing Mabli to the floor, for the metal would not break. In doing this, he got a closer look at her wings. Her wounds had not healed nearly enough to hide the fact that she had been sliced open to allow the wings through. Xavier grabbed one of her emerging wings and tried to rip it from her body, but Mabli felt a pulse shoot through her body and send her father flying backwards. Mabli remembered how Dameon said the pendent would protect her.

"What is this?!"

Mabli stood and covered herself up. She tried to run, but her Father had already yelled out orders.

"You are never to see the outside light again, Guards!"

Three guards came running through the palace doors.

"Take my daughter to her room. She is to stay inside. Do not let her out for any reason."

Mabli was screaming at the top of her lungs as the guards dragged her away.

"YOU CANNOT STOP ME FATHER! I WILL BECOME ONE OF THEM! I WILL!"

The King collapsed into his throne. Mabli was pushed into her room and the door was slammed and locked behind her. She pounded on the door for only a moment. Then she calmly slid down to the floor. She wept for a moment before her head snapped up. Mabli went to her closet and pulled out a red cloak. She threw it over herself, placed the hood over her face and started to climb out of her window and down a tree that was placed there as an escape route for her.

"Okay, he has seen me. He knows I am alive. He knows more than I would like, but now he cannot possibly blame Stocking for my disappearance."

King Xavier sat on his throne.

"She has wings."

He put a forkful of food in his mouth.

"She has wings…those faeries are taking my daughter! Zindel had better hurry back with that staff. The sooner I destroy the faeries, the better off my kingdom will be!"

# Chapter Twenty-Seven:

## The Bitter Beauty Dryad

The next morning, when Zindel awoke it was foggy. Regardless of the fog however, Zindel could see Kyle clearly. He was starring off into the forest around him. His eyes were red. It looked as though he had not blinked in some time. Zindel walked over to him. Kyle watched Zindel come toward him. He looked at Zindel, as a child would watch his father.

"Tell me Zindel, is there anything that can be done to make them stop? Is there anything at all that will let me sleep again?"

Zindel looked sadly upon Kyle.

"Leave the realm of the faeries and they will leave you alone. However, you can never return. You will never be able to sleep in these woods ever again."

Kyle looked as though he would cry.

"Zindel, I do not know the way back."

Zindel nodded.

"I know. Chances are that by now the faeries have changed everything around anyway to confuse us if we chose that path."

"What am I to do?"

Zindel could not think of any solution to this problem. He could not turn the quest around for one man who chose not to listen to him in the first place. He had Princess Mabli to think about.

"All I can suggest Kyle is that you try your best to hold out until we make it back to Wyveren."

Kyle could not say anything. One tear rolled down his cheek. He wiped it away in a hurried manner. Why had he touched the faerie? Why could he not have listened to Zindel? Why didn't Zindel tell them exactly what would happen if any one of them touched her? It was mainly Kyle's curiosity that drove him to do such a thing. Zindel could have prevented that all with one more sentence in his explanation; and now that Zindel got him into this mess, he was not even going to turn the quest around and help him out of it. It would only be a few days lost going back to the outskirts of Wyveren. Kyle could find his way even from the Elvine Forest, but no. Zindel was doing this to punish him.

The other men were beginning to stir. Gwynn remained the last to wake. At the river that morning, Gwynn had washed his hair and was in the process of bathing the rest of himself. He had actually kept some of the mud from the day before and slept with it on his face. Zindel was getting impatient waiting for him, but it was Kyle who suddenly screamed at him.

"Gwynn are you almost through?!"

Gwynn looked up from his reflection in the water.

"Almost, Kyle you can not rush beauty. It takes hard work and patience."

Zindel decided to show some of his anger now.

"Well Gwynn, the human race may diminish, but at least you will have a pretty face."

Gwynn smiled at Zindel, clearly missing the anger and sarcasm in his voice.

"Thank you Zindel. It takes a real man to compliment like that."

Gwynn turned his attention back to his reflection in the river. Zindel was about ready to pounce on him. Owen held him back with a smile on his face. Then he placed his hand above his eyes as though he was blocking out the sun.

"What is that?"

Gwynn was lost in his beauty treatment. Other men followed suit of Owen trying to see what he saw.

"Hey Gwynn there is a bear up stream, defecating. Is that good for your face?"

Gwynn stood up fast and walked away. They were finally moving again. Zindel was a little concerned with the fog. This entire quest the weather had been with them. How would they know where they were going in such weather?

"Look at that horse over there."

Cole had pointed this out. Zindel looked in that direction. Sure enough, it was a shaggy brown horse. Once the men spotted the horse, he started to make his way over to them. Morgan squealed with delight.

"Do you think he will let us ride him Zindel? My feet hurt like nothing I have ever felt before."

All the men started to issue similar complaints. Zindel turned toward the horse as it stopped in front of him.

"We will take no rides today."

The horse then simply turned around and walked away eventually disappearing. The men all stared at Zindel. Kyle had a steady trot right up to Zindel and went to punch him in the nose, but he swung and Zindel dodged it.

"Listen men that was not a horse. That was a Pooka and its only purpose was to get all of us men incredibly lost. The Pooka will invite the unwary to ride him then he would drop off his riders in a swamp or a bog. There we may be prey to phantom lights, which are creatures that will lead us farther into the swamp to our death."

His men grumbled slightly but kept moving onward. After a little while longer, Cole's voice rang out through the men.

"Zindel, I think we have past that sink hole already."

Zindel stopped and turned to look at his men.

"Does anyone else agree?"

Slowly every man raised his hand in the air. Zindel sighed and sat on the ground. He motioned for his men to do the same.

"There is no use in walking if we are going in circles. We shall just have to wait for the fog to clear."

Kyle was still standing, his arms were crossed, and he was glaring at Zindel.

"So we are just going to sit around for a day because of fog!"

Zindel looked at Kyle and stood to meet him.

"Kyle, I realize that you are in a hurry to get on with this quest, but save the strength you have. It will not do any of us good to walk around in circles."

Kyle sat down but he was not happy about it. Zindel also sat down again. He looked around. Gwynn had taken out a piece of parchment and a quill pen. Kay had also noticed Gwynn.

"Gwynn, what are you doing?"

Gwynn looked thoughtful for a moment.

"I am drawing a map. We are lost, so I am helping. I am not just a pretty face you know."

Owen gave a look of surprise.

"Really?!"

Gwynn smiled.

"No, I have muscles too."

Kay laughed and Braen scowled. He turned his attention to Zindel.

"Zindel, how many evil faeries are there?"

Zindel placed his hand to his face and rubbed his forehead.

"Well, there is Velelia; she is the only truly evil one, and not truly a faerie. Mouyra is…misunderstood."

Braen wanted to know more.

"What do you mean she is misunderstood?"

Zindel repositioned himself on the ground.

"Well, Mouyra and other's like her used to live in ponds and rivers that nobody could find. Until one day, a couple of humans wandered out to them. Mouyra made herself scarce, not sure how to feel about them. After a while, those humans came back. This time Mouyra made herself known. Her appearance terrified the humans and they left in a hurry. A fortnight later the humans came back with a village of people, pulled about every faerie out of the water, and killed them. Mouyra felt responsible for the death of her friends. She fled her home and she vowed to punish every human who helped in the killing of her family. Though she gets confused and thinks that any human there to swim or fish is there to find and kill her, so she does it first. A number of people claim to have seen their friends being pulled under water while fishing or swimming."

Morgan and Dagon looked at each other.

"We'll have to be careful while fishing."

Zindel chuckled at them and Braen pushed for more information.

"Are there any more misunderstood faeries?"

Zindel sighed.

"There is also Numma, or the Bitter Beauty Dryad. She is supposed to be a being of perfect proportion and beauty. Nothing else comes close to it on earth, or the Faerie Realm. Gods and men alike desired her, though she rejected them all, for none were as perfect as her self was. Over time Numma grew so obsessed with the imperfections of human men that she vowed to punish all who crossed her path if they had so much as one hair our of place. Dryads however do not live forever. I have heard that Numma has squandered her youth looking for perfection and now she is old. According to legend, those who attempt to look for her have seen her as she was in her youth because of her magic; and those who try to make contact with her never return."

Owen laughed heartily and hit Gwynn who had been very attentive during this explanation.

"Well Gwynn, sounds like you finally met your match."

Gwynn looked at Owen.

"Why would you say that?"

"Well, you are to perfect for anybody and so is she."

Gwynn laughed, but Zindel suddenly sat forward.

"Now wait a minute Gwynn, Owen may be onto something."

All the men looked at him.

"No, I can not risk it."

The men pushed him for information.

"Well, I was just thinking that if Numma, well she is our link to the evil faeries, she's knows their business. If we could just talk to her we may not have to talk to them ourselves."

Gwynn seemed unimpressed.

"What does that have to do with me?"

Zindel shook his head.

"Well I was thinking that perhaps Numma wouldn't find an imperfection with you, and maybe she would talk to us or you at least. But I can not take that risk Gwynn."

Cole looked from Gwynn to Zindel.

"What is her lure Zindel?"

Zindel looked at Cole and thought for a moment.

"I believe it is love poems."

Gwynn suddenly pulled out a new piece of parchment. Zindel watched him for a moment.

"What are you doing Gwynn?"

"I am writing a love poem."

Zindel's eyes grew very wide.

"Why would you do that? You will lure her right to us. There are no known survivors!"

Gwynn looked up at Zindel and smiled.

"There will be this time Zindel, I am perfect."

Gwynn looked down and wrote a line of poetry. He looked up and something in the distance caught his eye. He wrote another line and the figure came closer. He wrote a third line and when he looked up he saw the most beautiful creature he had ever seen in his life. The other men were caught up in conversation.

"Don't worry Zindel, he can't write a real poem. It takes more than a pretty face and muscles."

Gwynn watched as the creature beckoned him toward her. Gwynn stood as if on command. Zindel looked at him.

"Gwynn are you okay?"

Gwynn did not take his eyes off Numma.

"I'm fine, just going to have a piss."

Zindel accepted this and went back to his conversation with the men.

"I heard once, that Numma's voice breaks her magical spell and reveals her the way she looks in her old age. That is why she never speaks a word. Others have said that she is waiting for her true love before she will speak again."

Gwynn walked toward the beautiful creature. They were in the forest away from the sight of the group. Gwynn went to touch her but she moved away. Gwynn spoke to her.

"Who are you?"

She stayed silent.

"You are the most beautiful creature I have ever seen."

Numma went to touch Gwynn's hair. She was at a loss; she could not find a single imperfection with him. Could it be that she had finally found the one person worthy of her beauty? Her eyes softened.

"I am Numma."

Gwynn suddenly watched as this beauty before him faded into her true age. Her wonderfully full, luscious, shiny brown hair turned into a pasty thin-layered white. Her toothy luminous smile turned a horrid black mess with gums. Her baby soft face had so many wrinkles in it now that Gwynn could not count them. Even her vivacious green eyes had lost their luster; they had a kind of cloudiness to them now. Gwynn made a face of disgust and turned to walk away. Numma hobbled in front of him to stop him from leaving. Gwynn pushed her aside and started his way back to the men. Numma was mad now. She grabbed Gwynn and dragged him deep into the forest. She was surprisingly strong for such an old Dryad. Gwynn made to scream or make any kind of sound to let the others know, but he was silenced. Zindel looked behind himself in the direction that Gwynn had taken off in.

"That is an awful long piss."

Kay commented.

"Maybe he got lost."

Owen stood with a sense of urgency.

"We should go look for him."

Zindel and all the men ventured out. They did not have to go far. They found Gwynn sitting against a tree, covered in blood. They all ran to his side. He could only utter one word.

"Numma"

Then he fell over from the tree and died.

# Chapter Twenty-Eight:

## Journey to the Brizilyant Forest

The men gave Gwynn a proper burial and stayed the night at his gravesite. Zindel's dreams were plagued with thoughts of Numma. Faeries were never that violent. They would never know what Gwynn had done to provoke her. Then again, Gwynn was the only person ever to be found after an encounter with the fair Numma. Perhaps this was what all of her victims faced. Zindel was so sure that Gwynn would the one person Numma would not attack. Even though it was not Zindel's ideal to bring her forward, he had still put the ideal into the heads of the other men. Zindel awoke to find Kyle staring angrily in Zindel's direction. He stood and walked over to him.

"How was the night Kyle?"

Kyle glared at Zindel before giving an answer.

"I suppose you wouldn't know, since you were sleeping and all."

Zindel should have expected an answer like this. He turned and sighed. Kyle was getting worse. Zindel was doing some calculations in his head and the answer did not come up to his liking.

"Kyle, I am sorry. How about you accompany me down to the river? We can fill the water pouches of all the men and head out early."

Kyle gave a smile that could match Braen.

"Sorry Zindel, I must save what little strength I have. Looks like you are going alone."

Zindel sighed again, took up the men's water pouches, and walked down toward the river. When he returned the men were already cooking breakfast. Kyle was standing around and barking orders at the men.

"Why do you always over cook the damn rabbit?! How do you expect us to eat that rubbish when we can hardly chew it? Swallow it whole? Well I don't know about you Erwin, but I have teeth and I generally like to use them!!"

Zindel asked one of the men standing close to him.

"Kay, what is going on here?"

"I don't quite know Zindel. I got up and started the fire as usual this morning and when the hunters came out of the woods Kyle started screaming at all of us. I think Gwynn's death must have affected him the most. None of us men are saying anything about it, out of respect for Gwynn. Poor Kyle, I never knew he and Gwynn were that close honestly."

Zindel was not going to correct the assumption. It was a good explanation that none of the other men would question. Zindel walked over to Kyle after he finished bellowing at Erwin, and pulled him aside.

"Kyle, I know that this is because you haven't been able to sleep, but it is not anybody else's fault, so let up a little."

Kyle pulled his arm out of Zindel's grasp so fast that he actually lost his balance for a moment. He steadied himself before he whispered to Zindel.

"That is right Zindel it is not anybody else's fault, but yours! All you had to do was tag on that the faeries would never let you sleep again and I would have stayed away! I never would have touched her if you had told us all properly what would happen!"

Zindel had half a mind to set Kyle straight, but decided that this was a losing argument. At least while Kyle was in this frame of mind. The best thing to do would be to let him be angry and get over it. The men set out again after breakfast and Braen wasted no time being impressed with Gwynn's death. Owen and most others were silenced by his death. Kyle was angrily starting to mutter things beneath his breath, which left Kay and Cole the only two talking amongst themselves. Zindel had one goal really, and that was to get to Velelia or Mouyra, though he wanted to visit neither. Braen suddenly found his voice and began to question Zindel once again.

"Zindel, you said that Numma was misunderstood. She seemed to know exactly what she was doing."

Braen turned to face Kay and Cole.

"Did you see what she did to Gwynn!?"

Owen suddenly came out of his silent retreat.

"We all saw Braen, and if you are not careful, I will do the same to you!"

He drew his sword and pointed it toward Braen. The group of men circled around them. Zindel came bursting through.

"Owen! Put your sword away we have enough on our hands without you two going at each other."

Owen slowly put his sword back in its holster.

"Zindel, if he says one more gloating detail about how Gwynn died, I will not be responsible for my actions."

Zindel turned toward Braen.

"Neither will I."

Braen caught the message. He walked on.

"Where are we headed Zindel?"

Braen whined. Zindel looked at him as he walked.

"To find Mouyra or Velelia, whomever we come across first."

Braen pushed for more information.

"How do you lure them?"

Zindel sighed before answering.

"For Mouyra, someone will have to be near the water. For Velelia it is the simple trespass of her domain and she will find us."

"When is it that we will get to her domain Zindel?!"

Braen asked not bothering to hide the excitement in his voice. Zindel answered reluctantly.

"The last I heard, she was in the Brizilyant Forest."

Cole piped up suddenly.

"I've never heard of that forest Zindel, is it close?"

"We shall reach it in a day or so."

Braen smiled. They walked for that entire day with only one stop for a midday meal and water pouch refills. Kyle was again barking orders at those who had cooked the rabbit that morning.

"I have chewed this piece for five minutes now and I still can't swallow it. I vote on somebody else do the cooking tonight."

Kyle was getting ruder and ruder by the minute. Zindel once again tried to talk to him at the midday break.

"Kyle, they are starting to ask questions. You must try and constrain yourself."

Kyle began to laugh uncontrollably.

"That…ha ha ha…is the…ha ha…funniest…ha ha ha… thing I…ha ha…have heard…ha ha…since this…ha…quest started!"

Then his laughter died as sudden as it had come.

"Zindel, you are leading us to NOWHERE! HOW MANY MORE MEN HAVE TO DIE FOR YOUR STUPID QUEST?!?"

Kyle was now yelling and the entire group of men was just starring at him. Kyle did not notice this however and just stood there looking dumbly at Zindel. Zindel simply placed a kind hand on Kyle's shoulder and leaned in to whisper in his ear.

"I hope you will note dear boy, that this is not my quest. We are searching for the Golden Staff of Enchantment to save the Princesses life. A quest which you willingly volunteered for, do not call me out Kyle, for a decision you made on your own."

Zindel then turned and walked away from the weak boy. Who fell to the ground and burst into tears the moment Zindel let go of his shoulder. Trent walked up to Zindel.

"What is wrong with my brother?"

Zindel glanced back at Kyle before turning to Trent.

"He has experienced far too much loss in too short of a time. Bevyn, Razial and now Gwynn; Kyle is not one who takes to change and this quest was nothing but change for him. I am afraid that Gwynn's death was the final straw poor Kyle could handle."

Trent looked scared for his brother. He was thinking hard about something.

"Perhaps I should take my brother and turn back for Wyveren."

Zindel quickly shook his head at this suggestion.

"I have talked with Kyle about going back. He too thought he should, but I would not let him or you go by yourselves. It is too late anyway the faeries would have rearranged everything around by now."

Trent looked onward at his brother. Then spoke without breaking his glance.

"What can we do Zindel? For Kyle I mean."

Zindel took a deep breath.

"Not let anybody else die. Just try to keep everything as similar to right now as can be throughout the remainder of the quest."

Trent nodded and then went to help his little brother off the ground. When they came to the camp that night Trent himself looked fed up with his own brother. He placed him on the ground and walked away without a word. The other men gathered around Kyle.

"Kyle, is everything okay?"

"GET AWAY FROM ME! LEAVE ME ALONE!"

Zindel beckoned everyone from Kyle and made camp a few feet away. All the men eventually fell asleep that night around the warm campfire. Kyle was sitting straight up and shivering. He did not even bother looking at anything in particular, just starring straight into nothingness.

The next morning the men had eaten their breakfast and filled their water pouches the entire time it took Kyle to stand up. Trent took the liberty of filling his brother's pouch and making sure he was actually eating on the move. He

literally had to put the piece of rabbit in his brother's mouth
and tell him to chew. Things were moving slower than usual
because of this. They did not cover nearly as much ground
as Zindel had hoped they would that day. It was not until
midday break that everyone began to suspect that Kyle was
far worse than they had previously thought. All the men put
their things down and Kay went to light the fire for lunch.
The hunter's took off, the watermen took off with the men's
pouches and Zindel, and the others sat around and waited
when Kyle stood and started speaking.

"Damn bird. Can nobody else hear that loud ghastly
thing?!"

The men could not. The most sound they could hear was
the river running about a half a mile out. They looked at each
other with concern. Kay glanced at Kyle cautiously.

"In what direction is the bird, Kyle?"

Kyle turned around and looked at Kay. Thought for a
moment, but did not say anything at all to him. Kyle simply
turned around again and starred into the trees near by. Kay
turned toward Zindel.

"Is this a normal part of grief?"

Zindel nodded. Though he was not sure how much longer
he would be able to keep up this lie. Kyle suddenly turned
around again and directed a comment at Kay.

"I can't see the bird. I can only hear it. It is loud
though."

Kyle then placed his hands over his ears and sat down
facing the trees. After lunch, Trent picked up Kyle's water
pouch and a handful of rabbit that Kyle did not eat again
and placed the food in his mouth as they walked. Kyle was
more talkative this time. The men were walking along quietly

and Kyle started to scream for no reason that they could see. They all stopped and turned to look at him with alarm.

"THAT DAMN BIRD!!!"

Kyle pulled one of his arrows out of his sling and loaded onto the bow then started turning in circles aiming upward toward the trees. The arrow fell off for he was not holding it on, but Kyle's actions were enough for all the men to start to back away and Kyle kept on talking.

"I'm going to kill it! First I am going to find it, then kill it and just for the fun of it eat it!"

Trent turned toward Kyle. He grabbed his baby brother by the shoulders and forced him to look in his eyes.

"Kyle, what bird?!"

Kyle seemed shocked. He looked at his brother almost with hurt in his eyes.

"How can you not hear that racket? It is terrible! And what's worse is I think it is following us…"

Kyle suddenly lowered his head as though he was connecting something very important. He then snapped it up and looked at Zindel.

"Zindel! I believe it is an evil faerie! It is Velelia in the form of a bird! She is following our trail and we will all be transformed!!!"

Zindel shook his head with dismay at all the other men.

"She does not leave her territory and we are still half a day out from it. Also Kyle, no one else can hear this bird."

Kyle suddenly drew a look of confusion on his face.

"Potatoes aren't in season. Throw apples into the river! The fish swim in the air!! THE FISH SWIM IN THE AIR!!"

All the men looked at Kyle with dismay. What was he jabbering on about now? First, he was hearing things and now he was spouting gibberish. Trent looked at Zindel.

"Clearly this is not grief. Something has been done to him!"

Zindel could see no way out of this except the truth.

"What was done to him, he did to himself."

Trent looked at Zindel for a further explanation. Zindel looked around at all the other men before sighing and taking a seat on the ground. The men all followed his example except for Kyle. He started to look at all the men and then started to scream more nonsense at them. Eventually starting into a hysterical sob and falling to the ground to cry. Zindel started to talk.

"The night we found Lucille was when this spell was placed on Kyle. While all of us were sleeping, Kyle went back to her. He disturbed her eternal slumber. Now, any man may look upon the beautiful sleeping Lucille, but any man who attempts to disturb her shall also be disturbed. The faeries have put a spell on Kyle that will not allow him to sleep."

Trent placed a hand on top of his brother's head.

"So he hasn't slept at all since we left Wyveren?"

"No, and he will not sleep in the realm of the faeries."

Trent fought back the tears in his eyes.

"He will die then?"

Zindel nodded his head.

"His chances of survival are small. However if we can keep him fed and watered, perhaps there is a chance we can make it back to Wyveren."

Trent picked up his things and looked at the other men still sitting on the ground.

"Let's go then. If there is a chance that we can save my brother then we must. We shall find this Golden Staff and return to Wyveren as soon as possible."

The other men all nodded in agreement and they all stood together, gathered their things, and continued onward.

# Chapter Twenty-Nine:

## The Brizilyant Forest

It was close to dusk, the time that the men generally stopped for the evening when Cole stated above the rest.

"Zindel! That is not our destination…is it?"

Zindel looked up and grimaced.

"I am afraid so Cole."

"But it is so dark. It is no wonder I have never heard of these woods. It does not look as if it issues survivors, and we all know that dead men can't speak."

Zindel threw is bag down and started to make as if he was getting settled. Trent looked at him from the back of the group while supporting his brother's weight.

"Zindel what are you doing?"

"I am making camp for the night like we always do at this time of day."

"But, Zindel the forest is right there. We should continue."

Zindel gave a heart felt look at Trent, he understood why he wanted to get a move on, but he could not endanger his men.

"This forest is a dangerous place during the day, and almost certain death at night. We will have the advantage if we wait until morning."

Trent sat his brother down on the ground next to him and walked over toward Zindel.

"But will Kyle have the advantage if we wait?"

"Trent while I do want Kyle to get back to Wyveren the real quest is finding the Golden Staff for Princess Mabli."

Then Owen spoke up, for the first time since he threatened Braen.

"Zindel, I say we continued. The forest doesn't look that large we'll make camp on the other side."

Zindel looked at all his men, their determination was growing. He gave a great sigh and picked up his bag. He drew his sword and continued. All the men followed his example, except Kyle who did not have the strength. He continued to lean on Trent and follow him. They entered the forest and they walked. They walked for a long while and Zindel was beginning to wonder whether Velelia had moved her domain when suddenly a great rumbling shook the earth and Velelia erupted from the ground right in front of the men. Zindel held his sword in front of him.

She gave an evil smile at the group of men. She had an olive skin tone with brown eyes and jet-black hair not resting past her shoulders. Her lips were as black as a raven's feather and her nails were three inches long, each with a sharp point on the tip. Zindel was taking Velelia's image in when he realized a little girl standing by her side. She looked familiar to Zindel, but he could not place his finger on where he had seen her before. Her lips were painted black as were her nails, but her eyes were blue and she had straight brown hair and a little bit of a pudgy face.

"Ah, and who do we have today?"

Velelia followed up with an evil giggle. She was watching all the men stare at her in horror. Zindel spoke without taking his eyes off the little girl.

"I am Sir Zindel a knight from Wyveren."

Velelia turned attentively to his voice and caught his gaze.

"Allow me to introduce you *Sir* Zindel, to my daughter, Stella. She is the first successful human to faeries transformation. She has been my daughter for the past ten years."

It suddenly snapped for Zindel. He knew where he had seen this little girl before; He had seen her, in Razial's face. Zindel did not want to let on that he knew.

"I seek the Golden Staff of Enchantment!"

Velelia smiled.

"As do I, *Sir* Zindel."

Zindel's face fell.

"Then, you do not have it?"

Velelia laughed and got a wistful look on her face.

"I wish I did then *I* could be the Queen."

Zindel advanced on her with his sword, but Velelia put up one hand and stopped him in mid run. He was frozen to the spot he stood. She walked over to him and talked directly to his face, allowing her fingers to play gently on his lips.

"Ah, ah, ah Zindel, I have heard of your past history with women, but I will not be easily seduced. Especially in front of my daughter—I must teach her the power of women you know."

She laughed a most horrible laugh and the little girl laughed right along with her. Zindel starred at Stella, wondering if she would ever be free from the evil surrounding her. Lightening bolts flew from Velelia's fingertips, one grazed Zindel's shoulder and another one hit Erwin square in the chest. Zindel's face filled with horror as he watched his son fall to the ground with smoke coming out of his ears.

"No! ERWIN!"

Zindel broke away from Velelia's magical hold and ran to him. Zindel scooped him up as if he was an infant and held him to his chest rocking him. Erwin coughed and Zindel released one tear of relief. He let that moment linger until he stood Erwin up and handed him over to Owen. Zindel got his sword to Velelia's throat before she could stop him.

"Tell me what you know Velelia and I shall let you live."

Velelia, with one of her fingertips, pushed the blade away with such force it sent Zindel flying backwards into his men. She doubled over with laughter.

"Zindel, *Sir* Zindel, you think you hold power over me?! Ha!"

Zindel stood with the help of his men, he knew she was right. He had let his men talk him into coming when they were at the disadvantage. How would they escape her? Zindel suddenly noticed a small wooden cage sitting at Stella's feet. Inside was a small brown field mouse with green eyes and a fluffy brown rabbit with blue eyes. Whatever happened, Zindel knew he could not leave without them, but how would he retrieve it? Braen suddenly ran forward and bowed at her feet.

"My Excellency!"

Velelia looked somewhat lost.

"What is this?"

Braen raised his head to look her in the face.

"I will be your eternal servant. I will do your every command. Whatever you ask of me, consider it already done your evilness."

Velelia smiled.

"Zindel, is this a joke? It's rather good actually."

Zindel did not answer but discreetly managed to slide his sword through the bars of the small cage and slide them behind himself. Zindel glanced at Kay who picked it up. Velelia chuckled at Braen.

"Tell me Boy, what is your name?"

Braen stood, relieved.

"My name is Braen."

"And you are terrified of Piranha?"

Braen did not even have time to look scared. He was already a giant fat rat in her hands. She took one of her piercing nails and sliced him open before dropping him in the river below, which she had summoned for this very purpose. Velelia watched as the water became alive. She smiled and laughed as she watched her newest loyal servant die. When Velelia turned around to face the men again, they were gone. Zindel had given the order to run and they did. Once they made it to the edge of the forest Veleia's voice rang out so every one of them could hear.

"What's the matter Zindel? Don't want to play? Don't worry I'll be here on your way back."

# Chapter Thirty:

## The Golden Staff of Enchantment

Mabli wandered around the village. She made her way toward the forest to meet her Prince. Her gown was torn from the climb down the tree though, and she could not go to him looking like that. She must have a new dress, but no one could see her either. She walked into a shop with her cloak low around her face. She found a dress she liked and went into one of the back rooms to change. She heard the front door open and two women came in. They were talking to each other.

"It is a shame about Princess Mabli, her being so sick and all."

"Yes, King Xavier had to send all those men on a quest for the Princesses Golden Staff."

"You don't think it'll be too dangerous do you?"

"Well, yes, what quest isn't? I do hope they return soon

with that Golden Staff for Princess Mabli. I hear she gets worse every day."

"Inches from death is the latest news."

"That poor girl."

The women left the shop after that and Princess Mabli came out from the back room, changed and ready to go.

"Golden Staff? I don't have one of those."

Mabli placed the money for the dress on the counter and walked out the front door with the cloak low about her face again. She made her way out to the forest. Once she reached the edge, she looked around her cautiously and walked in. After walking about a half a mile or so, she shed her cloak and started to call for her love.

"Dameon, where are you?"

"I am here Mabli, right here."

He revealed himself from behind a tree. Mabli ran to his arms and they held a long embrace.

"Dameon, my father knows! He knows what is being done to me, what we plan on doing!"

Dameon gave her a concerned stare and embraced her again. She leaned her head upon his chest and breathed him in. He spoke in a determined sort of voice.

"Then come, we shall finish tonight. You will never have to go back."

He took her hand and started to lead her away. Mabli stopped short however.

"Wait Dameon, there is more I have to ask you."

Dameon turned and stood facing her. His hand still holding hers, Mabli continued.

"What do you know of the Golden Staff of Enchantment?"

"It is in my Mother's possession. She created it when my *father* was banished."

Dameon's face was growing redder with this talk about his father. He clamed down after a moment however and looked at Mabli.

"Why do you ask?"

"Just now, in the dress shop, two women said that my Father sent several men on a quest to obtain it."

Dameon's eyes grew wide.

"Why does he want it?!"

Mabli shook her head not knowing what to say. Dameon came to a realization.

"He knows...he knows that if he gets it he can use our magic, he can kill us all."

Mabli looked like she was about to cry.

"No. He would not...he...he would. Oh Dameon what do we do?!"

Dameon thought for a moment.

"We must tell Mother."

Dameon took Mabli's hand to lead her away with him. She pulled her hand away from his.

"No Dameon. This is my fault. He is doing this because I love you. I have got to go and make him call off the quest."

Dameon came close to Mabli and placed her face in his hands.

"I feel like if I let you go, I shall never see you again."

"If you don't let me go, you may never see your world again."

Dameon pulled Mabli into a deep romantic kiss and then held on to her in a tight embrace. Mabli gently pushed herself away from him and looked into his eyes.

"I will come back Dameon."

Mabli then ran off in the direction of the castle. Dameon stood at the edge of the forest and watched her until he could see her no longer. Then he turned and headed in the direction of his own castle.

# Chapter Thirty-One:

# A Moment of Relaxation

K ay had walked about half a day carrying the small mouse and rabbit and he had done so without questioning Zindel. However, he felt his curiosity could not be silent any longer.

"Zindel, why did we take these creatures from Stella?"

Zindel decided to stop and rest anyway. What with Trent shouldering Kyle and he shouldering Erwin, with a hurt arm himself, they could use the break. Zindel sat and offered Erwin his water pouch before even looking at his own.

"We took the animals Kay, because they are Razial and his wife."

All the men studied the animals now amazement filled their voices.

"How did you know Zindel?"

Zindel satisfied that Erwin had enough to drink answered their question.

"Three ways really, Stella's face looks just like Razial's.

The rabbit had her same eye color and Tareedah said she had taken Razial to his family."

The men looked at the rabbit and mouse again with new curiosity. Awstin spoke for the first time in a very long while.

"What can we do for them Zindel?"

Zindel sipped from his water pouch before answering.

"When we find a faerie that will not run from us, we can ask them to help reverse the magic."

The men were starting to stand now. Zindel went to help Erwin up,

"Please Fa...Zindel I am fine now. I can walk on my own."

The men were walking toward a new forest called Loch Lomond. This was rumored were Mouyra was last seen. The men were quiet on this walk. Zindel broke the silence.

"Well, at least Braen died how he lived."

Austin spoke again. He was talkative today.

"How is that?"

"Worshipping evil."

Tristram also spoke out in the conversation.

"Who are we going towards now Zindel?"

"Mouyra, but we are still a few days out from her."

Kay was picking up a nice piece of wood on the trail for the campfire that night. He spoke as he stood up with the log in hand.

"Mouyra is the last evil faerie, right?"

Zindel had to think for a moment.

"As far as I know, yes."

Kyle suddenly burst out.

"Why are there clouds at my feet?!?"

The men all stopped and turned to look at Kyle. He was

now so weak he was barely able to walk. It was more like a stagger walk. He spoke again, but this time it was quieter.

"Why are there clouds at my feet?"

Trent sighed and then looked at Zindel.

"Well at least we can relax for a bit then."

All the men began to walk again. Trent gently pulled Kyle along with him. Zindel questioned Trent.

"Why do you think we can relax?"

Cole answered for him.

"Well, Trent has a point. If Mouyra is still a couple days out, and we have already passed through Numma and Velelia's domains, then we have little to worry about."

"It does not mean we are safe."

Tristram sighed. The most noise he had made this entire quest. Zindel had to turn his head to see who was talking once he started.

"When this quest is over, I am going home, not that anybody at home wants me back."

Awstin did not seem to register his comment and went on with the conversation.

"I hope we return before fall. It is the Princesses favorite season."

Trent's next comment was so full of anger and resentment.

"I hope we get to have another battle before this quest is over."

Zindel had to look back to see if his face matched his voice.

"Why would you need or want another battle Trent?"

"To get one of those *Faeries* that put this curse on my brother."

Zindel stopped short and turned around to come face to face with Trent.

"I told you once Trent, what happened to Kyle he did to himself. The Faeries were protecting their own."

Cole broke the uncomfortable tension.

"I miss my home. I miss the trees and the woods."

Kay followed Cole's gesture.

"I miss my bon fires every night."

Zindel finally broke eye contact with Trent and continued to walk forward.

"We have fires every night Kay."

"Ah, but not like this Zindel. Family standing around, food cooking, plenty of ale…"

Tristram spoke again, melancholy like.

"I have never done that with my family."

Again, Awstin seemed to ignore Tristram's statements.

"I miss my little hideaway. It has a stream with sunlight. My sister has claimed it for her own I imagine."

Tristram took the conversation back this time.

"I don't have any sisters. I don't have any brothers either."

Awstin finally seemed to acknowledge Tristram instead of talking over him.

"So you are an only child? You must get tons of attention from your parents."

Tristram reciprocated the conversation finally making him feel a connection with somebody on this quest.

"No, they don't really like me. I think I was a mistake. I have only made their lives miserable."

Kay joined into the conversation.

"Well, parents will be parents. How about a lady love? I will bet that she wants you."

Tristram started to stare at the ground as he walked.

"Well there was one, once. She left me though for, Gwynn actually."

Owen spoke for the first time willingly since Gwynn's death.

"I have a lady back home. Well I do not have her. I love her and I am going to tell her so when I return."

Zindel had to look back at Owen in surprise.

"You did not tell her before you left?"

Owen shook his head. Erwin looked back at Owen.

"I didn't take you to be the husband type Owen."

"Me either. She was that extra spice in my stew. I wasn't expecting her, but I can not see living without her."

Zindel smiled to himself.

"My wife was like that."

Awstin chirped back into the conversation.

"What happened to her?"

"Nothing really happened to her. I just can not see my family anymore."

Owen became brave now.

"Are they dead?"

Zindel paused trying to think of the best answer to give.

"They are to me. I will never see them again."

Cole piped up.

"It is not fun to never see your family."

Dagon turned his head to glance at Cole. Zindel spoke without thinking.

"Well, I will see them again, but I can not be with them."

Trent pulled Kyle along gently.

"Why is that Zindel?"

Zindel could have kicked himself for saying such a thing, but he had and now he had to answer for himself.

"I did something awful to my wife and my entire family hates me for it."

"What did you do?"

Trent countered. Owen suddenly came to Zindel's rescue.

"You really don't know when to stop do you? If he wanted us to know, he would have told us the first time we asked."

Zindel and Erwin shared an uneasy glance, though Zindel expressed thankfulness through his eyes to Owen and the men continued in silence.

# Chapter Thirty-Two:

## The Fire bolt Dream Faerie

The men continued their silent march for the rest of the day. They started to collect firewood for the fire they would have that evening. Zindel was toward the back of the group of men helping Trent with Kyle and Kay was heading the group. As Kay pulled back a piece of bushes that was blocking his view and his path, he came across a large oak tree. The shade and protection its branches would provide was too perfect to pass up. Kay dropped his logs and his caged friends and went about helping to build a fire ring when something caught his eye.

There was a jug of ale and enough glasses for all the men to drink from. Kay ran toward it. He had been drinking nothing but water this entire trip and his lips were craving some ale at this very moment. The others gathered around the beautiful sight and Kay was pouring the glasses and passing them around. Owen gulped his glass and was immediately holding it out for another. Cole sipped his lightly and laughed gingerly at everything else around him. Kay drank about half of his glass quickly, but had decided that he was going to savor the rest. Tristram was also sipping his glass, but seemed to be drunk already. Erwin grew brighter with every sip he took. Dagon clanked his glass against his brother's before tipping his head back and draining it. Morgan laughed and followed Dagon in the same manner. Awstin was happily talking with Seith and they were both sipping lightly on their drinks hoping to make the ale last.

By the time Zindel and Trent, leading Kyle, made it to the scene everybody had enjoyed at least one glass and was happily receiving a refill. Trent dumped his brother at the base of the tree next to the mouse and rabbit and grabbed an empty glass. Zindel curiously walked over to see what it was the men were drinking. As soon as Trent had tipped his glass upside down into his mouth and was happily replenished with a refill, the men broke out into song. They sounded as a bunch of drunken men singing would sound. Zindel reached the ale and sniffed it. He knew right away that there was something wrong. This was Faerie Ale. The men had drunk something that belonged to the Faeries and they were prisoners!

Owen and Cole began to dance, doing a type of doe-see-doe with each other. The others began to join them. They were singing, laughing, and having a wonderful time dancing in a circle around Kyle and the tree. Kyle was clapping his hands and appeared to be laughing.

Zindel looked around frantically. A Faerie must have trapped them for some reason, where were they? Suddenly she appeared sitting crossed legged on a tree branch was Aerella. Her giant red wings blended into the branches around her. Her creamy skin disappeared underneath her fire like clothing. Her raven black hair hid Aerella's blue eyes, which was about shoulder length. She smiled and waved at Zindel before she descended toward him.

"Zindel, is it truly you?"

Zindel was not too thrilled at his men being trapped, but he was cordial all the same.

"Yes Aerella, it is I."

Aerella smiled at him.

"I heard that you were questing in the Realm of the Faeries and I had to see for myself."

Zindel suddenly found his anger.

"How long, do you intend to hold them Aerella?!"

Aerella was slightly taken aback by Zindel's tone, but was quickly all smiles again.

"They do look like they are having fun Zindel."

Zindel was not amused by her playful banter.

"Who is it you are working for Aerella?"

Aerella turned her entire attention away from the dancing circle of men now to face Zindel fully.

"I work for no-one *your highness*. I simply wanted to see you again."

Zindel felt sheepish now. He had let his temper get the better of himself.

"I am sorry Aerella; I do miss this world so."

Aerella get sad.

"Why did you do it Zindel? Why?"

Zindel went to touch her shoulder but she flew back to her tree branch. She looked down upon him.

"They shall dance until midnight."

With that, she was gone. Zindel had not even gotten to ask her to help with Razial and his wife.

# Chapter Thirty-Three:

## Faerie of the Silent Silver Forest

A s soon as midnight had come, the men did stop their dancing and almost immediately went to sleep. Kyle stayed awake however and felt the cold of the night without the usual fire. When the men awoke the next morning, they were ravenously hungry, for they had danced right through dinner. Zindel lectured them as they ate their breakfast.

"Did I not tell all of you to never eat or drink anything from a faerie?!"

Kay spoke on behalf of the men, since he was the guilty party who found the ale and began to distribute it.

"Zindel, I never thought that the ale belonged to the Faeries. I did not know that they drank. To be honest I thought that some other traveler's forgot it."

Zindel tried to stay angry with them.

"Because of your actions, you all danced and sang until midnight in a circle around Kyle."

Zindel suddenly noticed that Kyle was not eating. He watched for a moment as Trent tried to feed his brother. Kyle would not even chew the food before it fell out of his mouth again. Zindel walked over to Trent.

"He is not eating Zindel I don't know what to do. He must be hungry, for none of us ate anything last night, yet he will not eat."

Zindel took the food from Trent and tried himself to get Kyle to eat. Kyle did not even blink, but instead let the food fall out of his open mouth. Zindel took Kyle's water pouch and put it to his mouth. He could drink.

"You will just have to keep him drinking."

Trent looked at Zindel with fear in his eyes.

"Zindel, without food, my brother will die!"

Zindel stood up.

"He will die much sooner without water."

Zindel was about to walk back toward the breakfast fire when he noticed Cole talking to himself over by a patch of trees. He changed direction and stood next to Cole.

"Whom is it you are conversing with little fellow?"

Cole smiled up at Zindel.

"The trees, I talk to them whenever we stop. Trees are so receptive. You know I live in one back in Wyveren."

Zindel remembered that fact being revealed during their guessing game.

"Love and respect for the trees is a good thing to have Cole. The Faeries appreciate them as well and many of them also live in trees."

Cole's eyes seemed to light up. Shortly afterward, the men headed out with Kyle and Trent trailing behind them. Cole was laughing and talking with Kay when he stopped short and started to leak tears down his face. There was a ring of badly burned trees all of them crisp and black. The rest of the men crowded around behind Cole and stared. They however were not starring at the burnt trees, but at the weeping Faerie sitting in the middle of the ring. Zindel spoke.

"Wilhamenia, is that you?"

The Faerie was startled. She turned around to look at the men who had been watching her. Her eyes settled upon the one little fellow who was in tears. Cole had not noticed the Faerie, he was still crying over the trees. Wilhamenia smiled through her tears and began to glow. She glowed so bright that the men had to shield their eyes from it. Once the bright glow subsided, the men looked up and all the trees were perfectly healthy and unharmed. Cole, who finally noticed the Faerie during her glow, was so happy that she had fixed the trees he ran over to her and he was going to hug her, but Zindel intervened.

"Do you see that pendant in the middle of her chest Cole?"

Cole looked up and nodded at Zindel.

"That pendant means she is a member of the Royal family. You must never touch a member of the Royal family without their permission."

Cole nodded at Zindel and looked apologetic towards Wilhamenia. He bowed as he spoke to her.

"Sorry if I alarmed you Miss, I was so overcome with gratefulness for what you did for those trees."

Wilhamenia smiled at the little fellow and slowly held out her hand for him to take. Zindel was very alarmed at this gesture. Cole looked at her hand with intensity. He slowly reached up to take it. Zindel spoke to him very frantically.

"Cole, do not take her hand. She will lead you away forever!"

Cole did not seem to hear Zindel at all. He was looking so intensely at this hand that had healed all the trees. He was so grateful; he wanted to kiss the hand of the healer of the trees. Zindel's voice finally reached his ears.

"Cole, what of your own little tree home? Back in Wyveren; you will never get back to it."

Cole then hesitated. How he loved his little tree home. Then Wilhamenia spoke.

"We can make our own tree home Cole. Never have I found another with such compassion for the trees. Come with me and we shall live together in one of the world's largest forest."

Cole looked back at the group of men with a huge smile.

"Dagon, I am sorry about Lucy. I never meant for you to lose her brother. I am going to miss you."

Dagon started to tear up, went over, and hugged his brother.

"Cole, I forgave you a long time ago. It is myself I need to mend things with. Not you; please don't leave…not now that we are finally speaking again."

Cole smiled at his brother.

"Morgan will help you to forgive yourself. I love you Dagon, but you have lived without me for a long time and… she is my Lucy."

Dagon released his brother and laughed while tears streamed down his face.

"Then I won't be your failed business. I love you Cole."

Cole then gently took the hand of the tree healer and

started to walk away with the fair Wilhamenia. Zindel suddenly cried aloud.

"Wilhamenia stop!"

She turned her head so that her brown bouncing curls danced on the wind and her blue eyes pierced right into Zindel's.

"What gives you the authority to tell me what to do?!"

"Because I am…"

Zindel trailed off his sentence. He had spoke without thinking and almost ruined everything. He sadly watched as Cole walked hand in hand with Wilhamenia deeper into the forest.

# Chapter Thirty-Four:

## The Sunrise Magenta Faerie

Zindel sat around the fire that night. He did not speak. The men tried to comfort him. Zindel knew that it was Cole's choice to go, but he felt that he had not done enough to stop him. Wilhamenia surely took Cole out of spite. With the exception of Kyle, who just starred blankly into nothing all the time now, Zindel was the last to fall asleep. He was also the first to wake in the morning. He was up just as the sun was rising; he went in search of the river. As he came out of their campsite, however he found Mawlee. She was sitting in a flower patch singing to the birds that surrounded her. She wore a dress made entirely of flowers. Her curly blonde hair was beginning to shine in the sunrise. She was completely occupied by the birds around her that she did not hear Zindel approach. She turned her head so fast that the flower crown she wore on her head slipped off to one side. She righted it as Zindel knelt beside her.

"Zindel, is that really you?"

"Yes."

"What are *you* doing here?"

"I am seeking something for King Xavier of Wyveren."

Mawlee laughed aloud. Zindel cocked his head to the side.

"What is so funny?"

Mawlee calmed her laughter enough so she could speak.

"The once almighty king Zindel is doing errands and favors for a peasant king."

Zindel did not smile.

"This is my life now Mawlee, do not mock it."

Mawlee stood from her bed of flowers.

"Honestly Zindel, I can do and say what I want to you."

Zindel nodded, he stood to face her.

"True enough. How are they Mawlee?"

She became very serious.

"You shall see them all yourself. Your quest will lead you to them directly I assume. You've already run into your daughter."

"Yes, she took Cole. I believe it was to spite me. How is Tessah? Is she still in pain?"

"How would you feel Zindel? You are wrong about Wilhamenia. She loves Cole. She has been waiting for him. Your other daughter showed him to her in a dream."

Mawlee suddenly looked beyond Zindel and ran. Zindel turned around to see Owen somewhat charging in his direction. His sword was drawn and over his head ready to come down on the Faerie. Zindel held up his hands as though to stop him.

"Owen! What are you doing?"

Owen stopped running.

"I thought you were being lured Zindel, I was coming to your rescue."

Zindel smiled to himself.

"No, I was gathering information."

Owen lowered his sword and re-holstered it.

"Can I ask you something Zindel?"

"Yes."

"Why is it that you can handle the Faeries while every other man has fallen to them?"

Zindel was looking around for an escape to this question. Suddenly Kay came running from the campground.

"Zindel! Owen! Come quick! It's Kyle!"

Both men forgot about the question and ran back to the fire. Kyle had his sword out and he was swinging it frantically in the air. The men were circled around him, but any body that got close would be in danger of his sword. Trent tried to grab him from behind, but Kyle turned the sword on his brother. Trent got out of there quick, and turned to Zindel.

"What has happened to him Zindel?!"

"I believe he has started seeing things that are not truly there!"

Suddenly Kyle stopped fighting and looked around at the top of the trees. Whatever he was seeing it was circling around him. He was following it closely. It stopped. Suddenly it was diving right for him. Kyle ducked and took cover! He got up again and looked around. It was nowhere to be found. He gave a sigh of relief when he noticed his hand. Something was moving inside of him. It had not disappeared, it went inside of himself! He only had one option left. The men saw him raise his sword again. Then they all saw Kyle plunge his sword into himself.

"KYLE!" Trent yelled.

It happened so fast that nobody could stop him. They all rushed him however, laid him down gently, and pulled the sword out.

Trent cradled his brother's head as tears came streaming out of both of his eyes.

"What have you done brother?!"

Kyle looked at Trent, really looked at him for the first time in days.

"It is okay Trent, it is okay. I can sleep now. I can sleep…"

With that Kyle took his last breath and closed his eyes for the last time.

# Chapter Thirty-Five:

## The Green Loch Faerie

The men buried Kyle that morning. They started out around mid-day. Trent was silent. Nobody tried to comfort him; he had a right to grieve. Zindel began to worry of something else. Owen was too curious; he had caught on to too much. They stopped for the night and went about their usual routine. Dagon finally spoke during their sit around the fire.

"Do you suppose we will ever see Cole again?"

Zindel looked up at Dagon and saw the sadness in his eyes.

"Only if you search the forests for him, he will not come back to Wyveren. You must know Dagon that he is happy. He went willingly."

Dagon returned to starring into the fire. His friend Morgan tried to comfort him. For he knew that Dagon was sorely missing the sea and fishing; and that fishing was the only thing that took his mind off of Lucy after she married someone else.

"Zindel, do you suppose we could stop at the next lake we come across for a bit of fishing?"

Zindel knew that his men were missing their lives back at Wyveren, but they had all volunteered to come on this journey.

"If only we could Morgan, but you know that each day we are gone our Princess gets sicker. For her health alone we must stay strong in our quest for the Golden Staff of Enchantment."

The men remained silent until morning. After breakfast Zindel glanced around the woods. They were close to Mouyra. They would be there by nightfall. They walked all day, stopping only once for a short mid-day meal and break. The men began to talk again after that break. Tristram and Awstin were surprisingly good friends considering how they started out. Erwin and Kay became closer friends since Cole disappeared. Even Trent was talking, which was good for he had not spoken a word since Kyle had impaled himself. Seith was a lot of comfort to Trent, being an older brother himself he knew how to relate to him and what to say; which left Owen alone with Zindel.

"So Zindel, to continue our conversation from earlier…"

"Sorry Owen, but I must climb this tree to get our bearings straight."

Zindel knew perfectly where he was, but it was a good excuse to not talk to Owen. He knew he could not avoid it forever though and eventually he would have to tell them, all of them the truth. Zindel purposely stopped them before they reached Mouyra's lake. At night, she would have the better advantage. The next morning Zindel awoke to find he was the last to do so. Everything was already going, the water pouches were filled, rabbit was cooking for breakfast, and the men were packing their bags. Morgan suddenly asked as they were eating.

"Where is Dagon at?"

Owen answered between mouthfuls.

"He went with me this morning to fill the water pouches, but when he saw the lake he got all teary eyed and said that he had to fish a little while. I figured that we were going that way and we would pick him up on our way out. I told him I would bring him some breakfast."

Zindel threw his rabbit aside, grabbed his bag, and ran down to the lake. The men followed his lead. Morgan ran with a panic to the front of the group.

"Zindel, what is it?!"

"That is Mouyra's lake!"

The men started to run a little faster. Awstin made his way to the front.

"Zindel what were her lures again? We have not set any out!"

"If you recall, she feels that she was pushed out of her homeland by humans. Dagon fishing there should be enough to make her angry!"

At that moment, they reached the lake and saw Dagon sitting happily on the bank of it with his man-made fishing pole cast out in the middle of the lake. He had his toes in the water. Zindel was happy to see him alive, but wasted no time.

"Dagon! Get out of the water!"

Dagon turned his head to look at them all and the moment he did his fishing string pulled straight and tight; so tight that it pulled the little man right out into the middle of the lake. Mouyra came up and grabbed the struggling Dagon down under the water. Zindel ran and jumped into the lake with his sword drawn. Mouyra rose to meet him.

"Let him go Mouyra!"

Mouyra eyed the sword pointed at her face. It was the same kind of weapon those other men had used on her family. She became very angry.

"Whose going to listening to you?! Who do you think you are coming into my lake and pulling your human weapons on me?!"

Zindel took a step closer to her, he saw Awstin jump into the lake. He needed to keep her distracted.

"You are still in the Realm of the Faeries and you cannot lie. Do you have the Golden Staff of Enchantment?!"

Mouyra blasted her magic and shoved Zindel backwards against a pond wall. The blow made him drop his sword into the water. He tried to grab it but Mouyra glided right over to him and grabbed his throat. She held him steady against one of the pond walls.

"No, evil is not at work on our end, this time."

Mouyra smashed Zindel's head under water and held him there with her slimy webbed hand. Her skin was a greenish color as though algae had been growing on her. Her hair was a brown that looked as though it had been coated in the muck that lay at the bottom of the murky lake. At that moment, a shadow fell across her face and she turned her brilliant green eyes upward to see Owen standing there. He took a handful of salt that Zindel provided for them at the beginning and threw it right in her face. She screamed and shielded her eyes from the salt, but nonetheless retreated. Owen jumped in the water and pulled Zindel up. Erwin, Morgan, and Seith helped to pull Zindel out. Owen retrieved Zindel's sword and returned it to a revived Zindel. As he looked around at his rescuers he noticed another group; while Zindel had been distracting Mouyra, Awstin found Dagon. Kay, Trent and Tristram helped to pull him out of the water and had been trying to revive him ever since. Zindel walked over to them.

"Is it too late?"

Morgan was crying and hanging onto Trent. Tristram slowly looked at Zindel and nodded his head.

# Chapter Thirty-Six:

## The Celestial Pure Heart Faerie

Morgan, in a fit of rage turned around and kicked Owen in the shin. Owen was extremely surprised, and started to hop up and down on his good leg while cradling the injured one.

"What was that for?!"

Morgan pushed Owen over so that he towered over him.

"You left him alone! It is your fault that he is dead Owen!"

Owen sat up so angry that he was face to face with the little guy.

"Now wait just a moment, if Zindel had told us that Mouyra's lake was right there, I never would have left him!"

Erwin came to Zindel's defense.

"I am sure that Zindel did not tell us for a very good reason."

Trent now stepped up beside Owen.

"Yeah, he had a good reason for not telling us about Lucille too."

Zindel's eyes softened into a sad expression. Kyle too had blamed him for not explaining further what would happen if anyone touched her.

"It is your fault that Kyle is dead Zindel! All you had to do was say exactly what would have happened and he never would have touched her!"

Now Zindel got angry.

"Yes he would have! The morning after he had done it I told him what would happen and he laughed and said *is that all?!*"

Trent then threw a punch at Zindel.

"You are a LIAR!"

Zindel stopped Trent's fist with his hand and then pushed knocking Trent over in a body slam effect. Seith ran immediately toward the two of them to pull them apart. Tristram was just watching the whole scene happen, when Awstin came up behind him.

"I will bet that you see this kind of thing at home all the time huh?"

Tristram turned toward him.

"How do you mean?"

Awstin could not take his eyes off of the fighting happening before him.

"You know, your mom and dad always fighting, because of you."

"They aren't always fighting because of me."

"Tristram, I live on your street back in Wyveren. Your folks are always hollering about how if you had never been born..."

Tristram punched Awstin; he did not hesitate at all. Awstin fell backwards but not for long. He came back at Tristram throwing punches and kicking. Kay went to help break up that fight. The scene was chaotic. Owen and Morgan were screaming at each other, Zindel had Trent in a headlock and Awstin was kicking Tristram on the ground. Erwin was trying desperately to break Zindel's grip, Kay was trying to pull Awstin away from Tristram, and Seith was trying to pull Trent away from Zindel; when all of a sudden a golden glow had come over everybody. Everybody's grip loosened, they stopped what they were doing and slowly turned toward the source of the glow. She was a tan Faerie, with golden curls. Long curls too, down to her calves at least. She wore a long dress spun from gold silk. She was just touching down on the ground and her large golden feather wings were beating gently to support her. Everything about this Faerie was golden, even down to her eyes. They were amber like in color. In her glow, the men all became calm and slowly walked towards her. Zindel recognized her.

"Deliah, it is really you isn't it?"

All the men turned their heads when Zindel spoke. They waited for the introduction to this lovely Faerie.

"She brings peace to conflict. All of us arguing brought her too us. In her glow we feel relaxed and calm."

Seith could not take his eyes off her.

"Not all of us were fighting you know."

He claimed calmly to the Faerie. She smiled back at him.

"I know and I am pleased to see that three of you were trying to keep the peace. I offer you three now the chance to come with me. We can live together as humans in peace and harmony."

Deliah extended both of her hands to all three of them. Kay and Erwin declined thankfully right away. Seith however was still starring at the fair Deliah. Back home nobody ever noticed him directly. Even on this quest, he was usually in the background, but this Faerie singled him out. She noticed him. She still held her one hand out to Seith and she was starring back at him almost as intensely as he was starring at her. With one final glance around the group of men, he placed his hand in hers. The men, still being in Deliah's glow, all happily wished Seith off. When they disappeared, however the glow did as well. The effect of the glow seemed to remain though. The men were calm and peaceful toward each other. Kay and Erwin talked.

"Why do you think he went with her?"

Erwin shrugged.

"I suppose because he was noticed."

Kay smirked.

"So what; I too was noticed, it did not make me want to take off with a Faerie."

Zindel popped into the conversation.

"Do you not remember Kay? Seith came from a large family. He was the seventh child born and one of the middle children. Being noticed was not something that happened much if at all in his life."

Owen pulled Zindel away from the conversation.

"Zindel, we need to talk. You have some explaining to do."

Zindel sighed.

"I thought I might sooner or later. Tomorrow Owen... tomorrow."

The men continued to walk, but only Zindel knew to where.

# Chapter Thirty-Seven:

## Plans Revealed

Mabli walked through the palace and found her father eating at his throne. He looked up and noticed her.

"Mabli! Come here this instant!"

He bellowed at her. She walked determinedly up to his throne.

"What are you doing out of your chambers?! What has happened to the guards outside your door?!"

"Nothing, as far as I know they are still there."

Mabli waited as her father took a bite out of a turkey leg before she continued.

"Father you have been lying to the entire Kingdom."

He paused to chew, then finished and started to drink. Then he looked up at his daughter.

"What do you mean Mabli?"

"I have not lost a Golden Staff of Enchantment. It belongs to the Faeries and you know it!"

King Xavier slammed his drink down.

"YOU SNUCK OUT!"

Mabli did not seem to hear the anger in her father's voice. She went right along with her plea.

"You cannot kill them father! I love him!"

The king calmed down slightly.

"You do not Mabli. He has clouded your mind with nonsense. You are a human, he is a Faerie, and it would never work."

"It will father!"

"His family will never accept you, just as I will never accept him. They are all better off dead anyway."

"If you kill them father, you are killing me too!"

The King chuckled slightly.

"You are not one of them, I have spoken with the doctor and this little wing mishap can be easily rectified."

"As of tonight, I am! If you kill them you are killing your own daughter!"

The Kings face drained of color.

"If you are one of them, then I have no daughter!"

Mabli brought her hand to her face as her eyes filled with tears.

"You don't mean that."

"More than I have ever meant anything. You have a choice to make Mabli. Live as a human or die as a Faerie!"

Mabli slowly walked to her room to pack her things. King Xavier sipped his drink and watched her walk away.

"She will never be fit to be Queen of my Kingdom. She must die."

He then pushed himself out of his throne and followed her to her room.

# Chapter Thirty-Eight:

## The Timid Lilac Bride

Owen had been patient with Zindel. Zindel was upset over the loss of Dagon but Owen needed answers to his questions. They were sitting around the fire that morning. Owen glanced over at the small grave they had dug the previous night. He nodded to himself; he had to do it for Dagon.

"So Zindel what is your wife's name?"

Zindel gazed into the fire, as if he had not even heard Owen.

"Zindel?"

Zindel came back to the present. He knew what Owen was looking for. He finally felt that he could no longer put off the inevitable.

"She *was* my wife. We are not married anymore."

Kay glanced up at this comment and decided to join the conversation.

"What happened?"

Zindel looked over at Kay now.

"We had an argument."

Trent had taken to not speaking to Zindel since their fight, but he could not pass up the opportunity to stick it to him again.

"Was she getting generous with someone else?"

Zindel looked at the smirk on Trent's face and something inside of him snapped. Zindel lunged at Trent. Another fight between them broke out. Owen and Erwin quickly went to break them up. Morgan sat silently watching. He had not said a word since they had buried Dagon. He did not even look surprised that a fight had broken out. Tristram had just come back from the river, dropped the water pouches, and ran to help break up the fight. The men had Zindel and Trent pulled apart, but they were still struggling to get to each other. It was only when Awstin spoke that they settled down.

"Does anybody hear that?"

All the men started to look around for the sound of the sweet song. Awstin started to walk in one direction and the singing became louder.

"Who is singing?"

He questioned. The men followed Awstin and they turned a bend and saw a tall slender girl sitting on a log. She had creamy iridescent skin. She turned her head slightly, unaware of her audience and revealed her crisp hazel grey eyes and tiny nose. Awstin watched her lips move to the song she sang. He could feel himself starring at this beautiful creature, but could not dare to look away from her. Zindel was starring also, he finally found his voice.

"She is the Timid Lilac Bride, but the Faeries call her Esabella. She is a member of the Royal family, the hopeless romantic. She plays matchmaker with humans, mainly through dreams."

Awstin finally looked away from Esabella and looked at Zindel.

"I know her. She is my dream Angel. Every night I dream of finding her, exactly as we just have. Except last night, last night was different."

Owen was peaked with curiosity.

"What was she doing in your dream?"

"She was talking with Zindel. They were arguing."

"What were they arguing about?"

"I could not hear what they were saying, but when she looked at me, her eyes filled with tears."

Kay suddenly joined the conversation.

"Why was she crying?"

"I don't know, but after she looked at me she ran to me and…"

Awstin was starting to blush slightly.

"She kissed you."

Zindel finished for him. Everyone looked at him. Esabella continued to sing her sweet song.

"Yes…how did you know?"

"I had the same dream."

Owen found this too coincidental.

"That is interesting Zindel. Why were you in Awstin's dream?"

"You misunderstand Owen; it was Awstin who was in mine."

Awstin turned back to Esabella, but questioned Zindel.

"Why was she crying?"

"She was trying to get me to turn back. To take all you men and go back to Wyveren."

Kay was confused now.

"Why would she want us to turn back?"

"It is because we are getting closer to the Golden Staff of Enchantment."

Owen began to raise his voice.

"So why are we not listening to her?! We have lost too many men already. Whose life are you risking by disobeying her?!"

Zindel turned to Owen.

"Your Princess is depending on us to find this Staff and return it to her. Her life depends on it."

Awstin was still looking at this Faerie.

"Zindel, what is her story? Why does she sit there and sing?"

"Esabella has no violence in her heart, only love. Love for one man whom she saw in a vision many years ago. She has been waiting decades for him to appear and finally he has come to her."

Zindel slowly turned and pointed toward Awstin. Awstin looked away Esabella in the silence of the men. It took a moment for him to register what Zindel had just said.

"Me? I am her love?"

"You came to her years ago in a dream Awstin. She has waited patiently and loyally for you to come to her. It is your choice to go to her now."

Awstin looked confused and bewildered.

"You will let me go with her Zindel?"

Zindel smiled at him.

"Esabella would never hurt you. She will be made a Human and live with you. It is fate that you joined this quest Awstin. However you must know that if you choose to be with her, you can never come back to Wyveren again."

Awstin looked around at the other men. Something was lacking in his life in Wyveren. No girl was right for him there. Not that there were not many to choose from. Awstin simply made no connections with any of them. Esabella though, he could not take his eyes off her or his ears away from her serene song. This was definitely a connection he had never felt with anybody else in his lifetime. It was not likely that she could be mistaken either. She had been waiting for years for him to come. He felt the longing in the dream kiss. He smiled at Zindel, nodded to the other men before turning his back on them, and started his walk over to his beloved singing Faerie. He stood in front of her now, she glanced into his face, and the singing stopped immediately. Awstin smiled at her and jumped up from the log bench and into his arms. Esabella kissed Awstin as she had in his dream and then hugged him so tightly. Zindel could see the joy in her eyes as she peered over Awstin's shoulder. She gave him a quick wave before they both turned and walked into the forest.

Owen was shaking his head as he watched them disappear.

"You sure do know a lot about the ways of the Faeries Zindel."

Kay seconded this observation.

"This is true. You have never been in direct danger from a Faerie when we other men have. Why is that Zindel?"

Zindel's moment had come. It was now time for him to stop putting off who he was. It was time for him to tell his men the truth. However, Trent's comment averted everybody's questions.

"Zindel, do you know who that is, in the woods?"

# Chapter Thirty-Nine:

## The Truth Revealed

O wen turned quickly to the direction Trent was pointing in and threw his sword automatically. The sword became lodged in a tree right next to the faerie spying in the woods. Owen's sword caught the faerie off guard, which only seemed to anger him. He pulled the sword out of the tree with amazing ease and ran toward Owen. Seeing that Owen was defenseless and weaponless Erwin stepped in front of him and drew his own sword. The faerie charged head on and Erwin and he fought. First Erwin, with his own sword pushed the faerie back slightly but he came back full force. He did a kind of spin and aimed the sword right for Erwin's mid section but Erwin ducked backwards low enough to avoid any impact. Erwin popped back up and swung his sword at the lower half of the faeries body, but the faerie easily jumped over the attempt. They both swung their swords now. Both were inches from tearing into the other when a resounding voice boomed over all else.

"STOP!"

Zindel had thrown himself between the two and both stopped just in time of hitting him. Breathless and a little shocked over what he had just done himself, Zindel spoke.

"Prince of the Faeries, is that you?"

"Yes, I have been following you."

Owen could not stay quiet any longer.

"Who is this Zindel?! Why do you know every faerie by name?! Why do all of the faeries, know who you are?!"

Dameon cut back into the conversation with a smirk on his face.

"I see lying has taught you nothing and that you feel no remorse for what you have done."

Zindel screamed back at him.

"I think about what I have done every day!"

Morgan broke the silence that had grown between Zindel and the strange faerie.

"Who are you?!"

The faerie finally took his eyes off Zindel and looked at the men now surrounding him. He re-holstered his weapon and kind of bowed his head.

"I am Dameon, Prince of the Faeries; Son of Tessah, brother to Wilhamenia and Esabella."

Tristram suddenly found his voice.

"Who is your father?"

Dameon looked at Zindel and gave him a smirk then turned to the man who questioned him.

"I am son of Zindel."

Morgan and Kay gasped. Tristram's mouth fell open in disbelieve. Trent began to laugh hysterically and Owen shouted at Zindel.

"I knew it!"

Zindel placed his face in his hands. All of his men knew now.

"Yes, I was King of the Faeries."

Dameon countered him,

"You still would be if you could have kept your hands to yourself!"

"Do not speak of that with me! You may be the future King Dameon, but I am still your Father!"

"I have no father!"

Dameon turned his back on the entire group of men and disappeared into the forest. Zindel was devastated. He slumped down to the ground and starred blankly into nothing. Tristram knelt beside him.

"Why aren't you king anymore Zindel?"

Slowly he began to speak.

"I cheated on my wife Tessah, a most horrible sin in the Realm of the Faeries. Even worse was that I lied about it. So not only was I exiled, I lost my immortality."

Owen, who was feeling on top of the world for not only suspecting, but in fact being right about Zindel suddenly felt ashamed of himself.

"So, you never got to see your family again—until this quest?"

"Yes, I have seen all of my children now and only Esabella has shown any kind of compassion. The rest hate me."

"Not all of them hate you."

Erwin interjected. He had been quiet until now. Zindel looked into his son's eyes and felt grateful that they were not starring back at him in anger.

Trent, who was still feeling resentful towards Zindel decided to interrupt the moment.

"Well, if you were my dad, I would hate you too."

Erwin smacked him in the head before addressing Zindel.

"Where do you go from here? None of the evil faeries have the Golden Staff of Enchantment."

Zindel stood up with a determined look in his eyes.

"I know who has it."

Morgan looked up at him.

"Who has it?"

"My wife has it. Tessah, Queen in the Realm of the Faeries."

Neither Zindel nor Erwin shed light to the fact that he also was Zindel's son. The men seemed to have enough disdain in finding out their leader's secret without adding more discomfort to their present company. However, it appeared that not even Dameon knew of his family relation. It was no surprise since Zindel was gone before either of the boy's were born. Zindel thought back to an old prophet, predicted even before his great grandfather's rein. That two brother's born of the same father would be the end to the Realm of the Faeries. Nobody ever took the prediction seriously because no king had ever been able to produce more than one son. Yet here was Erwin, full faerie stripped of his wings and forced to live as a human. Zindel was marching his second son straight to the place where he was born. He could not hide his fear that because he was bringing Erwin there he might be bringing to an end the only world that he ever really loved.

# Chapter Forty:

## The Queen of the Faeries

ameon walked up to Tessah and kneeled before her.

"He is still coming mother."

Tessah glanced over at her son. Her long straight brown hair fell below her shoulders and into her rustic brown eyes. Her features were very delicate and petite. Her small thin lips parted into a smile as she motioned for her son to stand.

"None of you children could stop him. He always was determined and stubborn."

Dameon stood.

"I fear he is coming straight here. Hide the Golden Staff of Enchantment. It is what he seeks. His king wants our magic to kill us all!"

"Zindel knows this?"

"Well, no. He thinks the Golden Staff of Enchantment was stolen from Princess Mabli, that she must have the Golden Staff to live."

"Did Princess Mabli tell him this?"

"No, she would never tell a lie. This is their King's doing."

"How do you know so much Dameon?"

"Mabli told me all she knew."

Tessah began to look around her chambers now. Dameon also began to look around confused.

"Mother, what is it?"

"Where is Princess Mabli?"

Dameon relaxed slightly.

"She went back to her father to make him call off the quest."

"She did what?! And you let her!"

Tessah had started pacing her chambers. Dameon started to look panicked.

"She said she would come back to me tonight."

"She may try, but if King Xavier finds out what she knows and that she might warn us...we may never see her again."

Dameon became very concerned.

"I cannot let that happen...I love her."

"And she is the future queen of our world."

"I must go to her!"

Dameon quickly started to run from his mother's chambers but he stopped at her door.

"Mother..."

Tessah stopped pacing and looked at her son.

"What if Zindel comes while I am away?"

"I will deal with him Dameon. Go and save Princess Mabli!"

With that, he left.

# Chapter Forty-One:

## Mabli's Fight

Mabli was gathering the last of her things from around her room. She had placed the last little keepsake that reminded her of her mother in her bag and she sat down on her bed. She closed her eyes and one single tear fell down from her face. She was leaving the only home she ever knew; where she was born, where her mother died. If she thought hard enough she could remember her last memory with her mother. Mabli was a little girl and she was dancing in a circle with her. Her mother was going to take her into the forest with her that afternoon. The Faeries had helped her mother get pregnant again. They were certain she was going to have a son this time. Her mother was laughing and singing about a son for daddy to complete their happy little family. Then her mother stopped singing and dancing, a shadow had fallen across her face and that was all Mabli could remember. She would not be so disheartened if only the last bit of memory she had of her mother's face had not looked so scared and frightened.

At that moment, a shadow fell over Mabli's own face, along with one of her feather pillows. King Xavier had pushed Mabli backwards and was now holding her pillow over her face. Mabli fought her father with all her might, her hand was reaching under her pillow where she kept a thick stick for her protection at night. The King started to talk to his struggling daughter.

"Don't fight it Mabli. You must have known that I was not going to let you live. Just be a good obedient daughter now and stop breathing."

Mabli's hand finally found the stick. She grasped it firmly and started hitting with all her might. Finally, she heard a loud clunk and the weight upon her lifted. She quickly threw the pillow off herself and stood up. She went to run out of her chambers but she was dizzy from not being able to breath and she fell, face down on the floor. The King got up and walked over to his daughter; he leaned over her and started to laugh. Mabli quickly turned herself over and kicked with both of her feet. She sent he father sliding clear across the room. He grabbed a sword that was lying under her bed and slowly stood. Mabli grabbed a sword from her closet. The King laughed.

"You have quite an arsenal in here Mabli. I wondered where my weapons were disappearing too."

Mabli was talented with a sword. She and Dameon had practiced on each other when they were younger, but she knew he would not hurt her so she was not afraid of him. Her confidence held strong with her father though. He moved and she countered beautifully. King Xavier could not hide the shock in his face.

"If I had known you could fight Mabli, I might not have been so bitter all these years that you were not a boy."

That comment angered Mabli and she ran at her father. They fought a good ten minutes before Mabli had him cornered. With the sword clinking and the battle cries from both ends, it was amazing that guards were not in Mabli's chambers. Mabli had no idea that her Father had placed all the guards appointed to protect her, in the dungeons after her first disappearance. She could not hope that anybody would come to her rescue. They were at a stale mate. Mabli had her sword across her father's throat, but he had his at Mabli's gut. The King smiled in spite of his situation.

"You will not do it Mabli. You could not kill me."

Tears started to trickle down her face but she held that sword tight as ever.

"You move, I move."

"No, you do not have what it takes to off your old man. I know you Mabli; you are just like your mother. She could not kill me when she had the chance either. She died just as you are about too."

"You killed my mother?!"

This truth was exactly what the King needed. Mabli faltered at this news and the King swiftly pushed his sword into Mabli's gut. She dropped her sword from shock and stumbled backwards, starring at her father's face the whole time; she finally tore her eyes away when her hands pulled the sword out and covered up the wound. The King laughed a hearty laugh as Mabli fell to the ground and started to bleed out onto the floor. Dameon charged through the door at this moment. He looked from Mabli to the King. In a moment of rage, Dameon pushed the King hard and he flew across the room and into the stonewall as though he weighed no more than a feather. Dameon went after him; he had picked the unconscious King up by his robe and started beating him. Then he heard a small cry. He released the King and went to Mabli's side. Dameon took the sight in. Her face was as pale as the moon and her white gown was covered in the puddle that was her blood. Mabli starred at him as though he was a stranger while she was gasping for breath. Every one she took threatened to be her last. Oh, if only he could move her to his world fast enough. There were healers there that could save her. He gathered her in his arms and held her. He began to cry. Mabli finally spoke.

"He killed my mother."

She lifted one of her blood soaked hands to his face.

"Dameon…"

Suddenly her breathing became unsteady, short gasping breaths before she went completely limp. Dameon squeezed his eyes shut and sobbed silently for a moment.

"No…no…NO!!!"

He looked back into his loves eyes and screamed at the pendant he noticed laying around her neck.

"YOU WERE SUPPOSED TO PROTECT HER!"

The pendant flashed, if Dameon had blink her would have missed it. Mabli's chest was rising with breath. It was slow. Dameon had to recall if she had stopped breathing at all. He was sure she had. After a few moments, Dameon looked Mabli over. There was color coming back to her face. He smiled at her and gently pushed some of her hair out of her eyes. Dameon kissed her forehead and noticed that she did not feel cold. He looked to where her wound was and noticed that she was no longer bleeding. He pulled the fabric of her gown apart and saw no puncture wound. Mabli started to come around.

"Mabli, how can this be?!"

Mabli looked herself and then she smiled up at Dameon.

"My power must be a healer."

Dameon hugged and kissed Mabli all over. He showered her with tears of joy for she was alive and at last a true faerie. He helped her up and they both fled for the Realm of the Faeries.

# Chapter Forty-Two:

## The Harmony Moss Faerie

O ut of the sixteen men who started this quest only seven of them remained. Not counting Razial and his wife, and Zindel was not even sure he could fix them. Zindel had lost a little over half of his men and he had only just discovered where the Golden Staff of Enchantment was hidden. Owen interrupted his thoughts.

"Where is the Queen located?"

Zindel continued to walk and look forward.

"I assume in the same place as when I was King. Why would she take the Golden Staff of Enchantment though?"

Kay answered him.

"Maybe she wanted you to come to her."

"Nonsense, she knows that all she would have to do is ask me, I love her."

Trent scowled at this.

"You still love her?"

"Yes. She is my wife; the mother of my children."

Morgan piped up now.

"You mean she *was* your wife."

"No, we are still married. I did not believe it before, but now I do. We have to be."

"How do you know there is not a new King?"

Erwin questioned. Zindel's face fell.

"Well, I do not come to think of it. She must be married. She cannot stay Queen by herself. The King and Queen share the power of all the Faeries. It is too much for one faerie to handle by them selves."

Tristram placed a hand on Zindel's shoulder.

"Maybe things changed after you left. Like you said before this is your first glimpse into the Realm of the Faeries in fifteen years."

"I suppose it could have changed."

Trent finally relinquished the scowl and replaced it with a smirk.

"Well that is easier to think of instead of your wife being in someone else's bed."

Kay rolled his eyes and spoke loudly at Trent,

"You know, Trent, some things do not need to be said."

Owen cut right back into Zindel.

"If you claim to love her so much, then why did you cheat on her?"

Zindel sighed.

"Tareedah came to me. She was mad and uttering incomprehensible words. She had just witnessed a memory of a human and collapsed into my arms in the woods."

"What was the memory?"

Tristram questioned.

"A man of wealth and distinguished background had brutally beaten and killed his wife right in front of their young daughter. The young girl ran into the woods and had distracted Tareedah. The girl was crying hysterically. Tareedah did not appear to her, but when she saw what the memory was she took it away from the girl. The young girl stopped crying immediately, stood up, and happily skipped away."

Morgan was horrified at this revelation.

"Who would do something like that especially in front of their young daughter?!"

Erwin showed concern also.

"What happened to Tareedah? Does she still have the memory?"

Zindel shook his head.

"No. The memory itself made her delusional. You see, Faeries are not generally violent. Therefore, when we witness something such as that, it does something to us. In order to restore her to her normal state of mind, I took the memory from her."

Owen spoke now.

"Well, when you took the memory, did it not have the same effect on you?"

"Yes, it did. I thought that because I was King I would be stronger. I was wrong, at first. I too became delusional in the beginning. I tried to think of anything but that memory. The only thing that drove it away was Tessah's face."

Kay now got defensive.

"How could you lie with Tareedah, when you could only think of Tessah?"

"Well that is just it. I was seeing Tessah. Tessah was Tareedah. With that memory still fresh in my mind, I did not know the real world from Tareedah's illusions. Tessah caught us together. I could never explain to Tessah what really happened because then Tareedah would be exiled for breaking the law."

Trent was curious now.

"How are you able to cope with the memory now?"

"Over time, and because I was King, I was able to keep the memory without being delusional. I think living outside of the Realm of the Faeries helped also. Humans deal with this kind of thing more often than they should. My living as a human all these years has helped."

Morgan looked into Zindel's eyes.

"Who was it? Who was the man?"

"You're King. King Xavier killed his wife and Princess Mabli was standing right behind him."

Erwin spoke now.

"Doesn't it bother you to know that you work for a murderer?"

"Every single day; but that is why I went to work for King Xavier. He must find it odd that Princess Mabli has no memory of what she saw. I work for him to protect her. To make sure he doesn't repeat his actions."

A small sniffle was heard behind the group of men. They all make an about face and are nose to nose with a faerie who has brownish-blondish curly locks and ocean blue-green eyes. She was wearing a burgundy flowing dress. Zindel was the only one who could speak.

"Deamone, what are you doing here?!"

"I was sent to follow you. Zindel, your highness, I never knew that side of the story."

"Yes I know. I never told anybody until now."

"To take a memory from a human is forbidden, but Princess Mabli will not be a human much longer."

Tristram spoke out.

"What do you mean?!"

Deamone looked at him and then looked at all the others before turning back to Zindel.

"She was always fated to be among us and now it shall be so. Mabli will be officially welcomed into the Realm of the Faeries, as soon as she comes back."

Zindel began to get all worked up.

"Who made that order?! Princess Mabli is deathly ill!"

Deamone smiled at him.

"Queen Tessah said you might say that. You are wrong Zindel in so many things."

Zindel took the small cage from Kay's arms and held it up for Deamone to examine.

"Can you reverse Velelia's magic on my friends?"

Deamone glanced at the rabbit and mouse closely.

"It is not Velelia's magic. It is Stellas. In either case, I do not have the power. I can see that they both have good hearts though. I am sure that Queen Tessah can help them."

Deamone began to turn away but Zindel stopped her.

"Deamone, is the palace in the same place?"

She stopped, but did not turn anything but her head to speak over her shoulder.

"Yes. You are heading in the right direction."

"Will I find the Golden Staff of Enchantment with her?"

"It is not as it seems Zindel, it is not as it seems."

Deamone disappeared. The men continued on more determined than ever.

# Chapter Forty-Three:

## King Xavier's Reason

E ven though Zindel knew exactly where he was going, it was not safe enough to travel at night. Not to mention his men needed their rest. They stopped in a valley between two sets of woods. Kay started the fire, Morgan and Tristram filled the water pouches. Owen and Trent went hunting for their dinner and Zindel and Erwin waited to skin, gut, and cook them. As they were all gathered and eating, Owen began to think aloud.

"Why did he do it?"

Tristram glanced up from the dirt.

"Why did who do what?"

Zindel answered for Owen.

"Why did King Xavier kill his wife?"

Owen nodded. Erwin perked up as well.

"I have been wondering that myself."

Kay was focused on the fire, but managed to speak.

"Zindel, do you know why?"

Zindel leaned forward toward the fire.

"I do."

Morgan suddenly turned his attention toward Zindel.

"Well…what happened?"

Zindel sighed.

"It was no surprise to anyone that Queen Cordellia was friends with the faeries."

Trent rolled his eyes.

"Obsessed with is more like it…" he paused for a moment, "Your people did something to her."

All the men were looking accusatorily at Trent. Zindel just cleared his throat and continued.

"However, not many people know that Queen Cordellia had complications while with-child, with Princess Mabli. It was unlikely that she could ever be with-child again."

Owen, who was listening attentively, did not know this about his late Queen.

"How do you know that about her?"

Erwin put the pieces together.

"You were friends with her."

Zindel nodded his head. Tristram voiced himself.

"She spoke to you about those kinds of things?"

Zindel again nodded. Trent started to laugh.

"It was not just Tareedah was it? You were more than friends with our Queen!"

Kay became upset, raged almost.

"You dare to desecrate the name of our late queen?"

Morgan remained looking at Zindel.

"Why would she confide in you?"

"It was not just I whom she talked with. Tessah was also there; almost all in the Realm of the Faeries were friends with her."

Owen sensed Zindel was trying to avoid the question.

"Yes, but why confide in Faeries?"

Tristram followed this gesture.

"Faeries do seem the least likely to keep secrets. If asked directly you cannot lie."

Zindel smiled now.

"True, but we must be caught before being able to have a question asked directly."

Trent now began to see Owen's point.

"Even if you were caught, you can dodge a question easily enough."

This comment pointed out to everyone what Zindel had done. Erwin pushed further.

"Why would the Queen confide such a secret in you?"

Kay followed up directly.

"She would not have wanted any one to know that."

Zindel sighed and conceded.

"She had to tell somebody. She was worried and afraid."

Morgan chimed in.

"Of what was she afraid?"

"It was no secret either that King Xavier desperately wanted a son."

Owen finally let up off the blame a bit.

"So Queen Cordellia was afraid of how upset King Xavier would be?"

Tristram nodded his head in agreement.

"I can see that, but I cannot see what she would gain by telling the Faeries."

Morgan silently mumbled to himself, but everyone heard him.

"She would gain sympathy."

Erwin shook his head.

"No, it was not that. She would have had sympathy from all in her Kingdom."

"Yes, all except King Xavier."

Trent blurted out.

"What could the Faeries give other than sympathy?"

Kay wondered aloud. Zindel went to speak but Erwin beat him to the punch.

"It was their magic."

Zindel nodded impressed. Owen leaned forward toward the fire now.

"So, you helped the Queen with your magic?"

"What did you do for her?"

Tristram questioned. Morgan spoke regretfully now.

"I am not sure I want to know what you did to her."

"You got her in the family way again, Zindel you are smooth with the ladies!"

Trent exclaimed. Kay stood up this time and threw his water in Trent's face.

"Do not speak that way about the Queen; to suggest that she would be with anyone but the King is treason!"

Trent was speechless. Zindel smiled now.

"Actually, that was exactly what we did."

Kay sat down in a slump.

"I can't believe that of our Queen."

"I knew it! I told you, all of you!"

Trent gloated. Owen knew better though.

"Shut up Trent."

Erwin spoke next.

"The Faeries helped her to get with-child again Trent; they did not o the act themselves."

"I thought the Queen was incapable of becoming with-child again."

Morgan pointed out. Tristram spoke directly to him.

"That was the magic. They fixed her."

Zindel took hold of the conversation again.

"It was not that simple. We did not fix her for good. This next child would be the last one she would ever be able to have. We helped her to become with-child again and we helped to make sure that this child was the son that King Xavier wanted so desperately."

Trent's curiosity was peaked.

"Why did he kill her then?"

"The King heard of her miracle. Queen Cordellia told him that she was to have his son after all."

"That does not seem to justify the reason of his actions at all."

Owen commented. Zindel continued.

"Well the King was told beyond a shadow of a doubt that the Queen would never be able to be having a child again. Xavier assumed that when the Queen learned this news she was unfaithful to him with the Faeries and that some of their magic had fixed her accidentally and she became in the family way again; and that she was trying to pass off this child as a rightful heir to his throne."

Tristram cut in.

"I never remember hearing of the expected second child of Queen Cordellia."

Erwin agreed with him.

"Nor do I, but you cannot expect King Xavier to spread that news around if he suspected that the child was not his."

Kay was pouting now.

"What proof did he have that Queen Cordellia had betrayed him?"

Morgan meagerly answered.

"Well, she was with the Faeries everyday using their magic so she could become fruitful again."

Zindel cut in.

"Other than her absence during daylight hours the King had no proof of any betrayal. He sat with the news of his son for a few days before he decided beyond a doubt that the child was not his."

"But the child was his, was it not?"

Owen stated decidedly. Erwin commented back to him.

"Of course it was. King Xavier killed his own future."

Zindel continued his tale.

"Yes, he went right into Mabli's room a few days later and beat Queen Cordellia until she could not fight back, then he stabbed her with a sword several times. He turned just in time to see Mabli run from her room."

"Then Tareedah found her crying in the woods and took the memory from her."

Kay added finishing the story. Zindel nodded. Several twigs snapped just then. Zindel and the others looked around. Then out of the darkness, a wolf-like creature lunged at the men and fell on Morgan. Morgan fought the beast horribly while getting bitten and scratched. Zindel grabbed his sword and stabbed the creature right through the ribs. It turned its head and gave a final growl at Zindel before it fell over and died.

# Chapter Forty-Four:

## Curse of the Full Moon

Zindel, horrified at what he just saw leaned over Morgan.

"Are you okay Morgan?! Can you sit up?"

Morgan moaned a bit.

"I am bitten and scratched; laying down feels so much better Zindel."

Zindel left Morgan to examine the creature. He glanced from his spiky fur to his sharp pointed ears. Zindel opened one of the beast's eyes and saw an amazing yellow. He pulled back the lips on the creature and discovered six extremely long and sharp front teeth. Zindel jumped back from the creature and quickly started searching the sky for the moon. It was behind a cloud. The moment it came out again, Morgan would be a danger to them all. Zindel withdrew his sword and walked over to Morgan. There was no time to explain, it was now or never. Tristram spotted Zindel and what he was going to do. He grabbed Morgan and held him close.

"What do you think you are doing Zindel?!"

The men looked at him, but before Zindel could say anything the moon light came out from behind the clouds and landed right on Morgan. The change was so quick Zindel could not even yell any warning to Tristram, who was holding onto him. Tristram was bitten until he let go of Morgan and then Morgan made a mad dash at the person directly in front of him, Trent. Morgan went right for the throat. Zindel lunged at Morgan and put his sword right through him has he had done to the first creature. Morgan snapped at Zindel once before falling over and dying. Trent was already dead. Zindel looked back in time to see Owen pulling his sword out of Tristram.

"Was anybody else bitten?!"

Erwin and Kay answered no at the same time. Owen was silent but he shook his head. Zindel was gathering his things. The others started to do the same.

"There was one and there will be more. We are not safe here!"

They headed out for the night. Nobody spoke until morning when they stopped for a bit of breakfast, though nobody seemed hungry. Zindel spoke.

"Once you are bitten this is nothing that can be done. There is no cure. Morgan and Tristram were gone the moment infected teeth pierced the skin."

Owen seemed to liven up a bit after this bit of news. Knowing that it was no longer Tristram he had put his sword through hours ago, but something that if given the chance it would have ripped him apart, cleared his conscience.

"The moment I get into town I am wrapping Amelia up I my arms and kissing her in front of the whole town. Life is too short to worry about what other people will say, or if the person will break your heart. Zindel, is the reason that you are never hurt because you were once a faerie?"

"No, I should be just as vulnerable as you. As long as Tessah does not forgive me, I am powerless. A faerie has no power unless they have someone to share love with."

Erwin cleared his throat.

"I believe you are mistaken Zindel. Not all the faeries we have come across have love."

Zindel nodded.

"You speak of Velelia, Mouyra, and Numma?"

Erwin nodded and Zindel continued.

"None of them are truly faeries. They live in the Realm, but they have no wings."

Erwin looked at Zindel.

"What about Tareedah?"

Zindel was silent for a moment.

"Without love, a faerie must borrow their magic from the King and Queen. Therefore a faerie has no power unless they have someone to share love with."

Kay looked up from the flames.

"Maybe Tessah sent you on this quest to observe you."

Zindel did not understand.

"What do you mean?"

Erwin explained.

"Well it has been fifteen years; maybe she is starting to wonder about you. About what happened to you, if you had changed?"

"Maybe..."

Owen chimed back in

"Maybe she has grown softer over the years. Maybe she is starting to let up a little."

"Tessah was always forgiving, but I cannot ask her to forgive me."

"Well Zindel, maybe she is waiting for you to ask." Erwin commented.

# Chapter Forty-Five:

## A Reunion Of The Heart

By mid-afternoon Zindel, Erwin, Kay, and Owen were standing outside Queen Tessah's palace with the caged rabbit and mouse. After a moment's pause, Zindel continued onward and the other men followed him. Zindel walked until he was face to face with Tessah herself. She sat regally on her throne with the Golden Staff of Enchantment in her hands. Zindel looked from it to her.

"Why did you take it Tessah?"

"I did not take it Zindel. It is you who is trying to take what is not yours."

Owen spoke behind Zindel.

"What does she mean by that?"

Tessah spoke directly to Owen.

"I mean that the Golden Staff of Enchantment is and always has been mine."

Kay piped up now.

"She is lying!"

Zindel spoke, but was not taking his eyes off Tessah.

"She cannot lie."

Erwin did not understand.

"Why would King Xavier send us after it?"

Zindel looked at Tessah.

"What is the importance of this Staff?"

"I brought it to power fourteen years ago. Many faeries were begging me to remarry and share the magic, for they saw the stress it gave me."

"Then you did not remarry?"

"No Zindel, I did not; for I still loved you."

Zindel looked away from her with shame in his eyes.

"So I brought this Staff to power and so it has been ever since. I can take the magic I need from it, without holding all of the magic at once."

Owen spoke again.

"Why would King Xavier send us to get it? I do not understand, he said that Princess Mabli would die without it."

"Your King has become aware of a potentially dangerous situation."

"What?"

Kay questioned. Tessah looked directly at him.

"That situation is love. You see Princess Mabli and Prince Dameon have fallen in love, and your King will not tolerate it."

Zindel smiled at Tessah.

"Dameon and Mabli are in love."

She returned the smile.

"Yes, she is being welcomed into the family as soon as she returns; if she is alive."

Erwin burst into the conversation.

"Why would Princess Mabli not be alive?!"

"Princess Mabli went to Dameon, telling him of the Golden Staff quest. He put together that King Xavier planned to kill all of us off with our own magic. Dameon came to me, but Princess Mabli went back to her father to try and get him to call off the quest."

Zindel was filled with emotion.

"We must save her!"

"Dameon has already gone to her. Though he has not yet returned."

"Well, the King is not going to let him go in and take her. He could be in real danger."

Owen commented. Kay followed.

"Come on Zindel, lets go save your son and our Princess!"

"It will take days to get back to Wyveren! Not to mention all the dangers out there. We left with sixteen men and four of us are still standing! Well five…and his wife."

Zindel held the cage up for Tessah to see. She took the cage from Zindel and looked at the frightened creatures,

"This is Stella's magic. It is strong but it can be undone."

Tessah opened the small cage door and the creatures stepped out. She touched the golden staff and then looked at the creatures. Before everybody's eyes, both the rabbit and the mouse became human again. Moments later, servants who eyed Zindel suspiciously brought robes to them both. Razial hugged his wife and held her there.

"Ten years Rosemary. Ten years I have been waiting to hug you again."

She hugged him back with tears in her eyes.

"I am sorry I did not tell you about the changeling. I thought you would think I had gone mad."

Razial continued to hug his dear wife.

"What about Stella? Can we save her?"

He directed this last part at the regal Queen. She started to shake her head no but Rosemary spoke first.

"Stella is not our daughter anymore Razial. The day I threw the changeling in the fire she appeared at our front door, just like she was suppose to; but before I could even hug her she changed me into a mouse and collected me in that cage and set fire to our house."

Razial was silent for a moment.

"When Tareedah took me to her, I thought…well I am not exactly sure what I expected to find—but it certainly was not our little girl—not my little Stella."

Razial was a little more choked up about it; Tessah spoke up.

"Stella was never supposed to become a Faerie. Velelia and Tareedah changed her. Then Tareedah intentionally led you to Velelia…she shows more and more evil with each passing year."

Erwin finally spoke.

"My mother is not evil…she can't be."

Tessah looked at him—really looked at him for the first time. She glanced from Erwin to Zindel and saw the minute resemblance between them.

"How could you bring him here?!"

Zindel sighed.

"I did not know until Tareedah crossed our path and by then it was too late."

Tessah's demeanor changed.

"You never knew? She never told you about your son's?"

Everyone except Tessah, Erwin, and Zindel gasped. Tessah glanced at them all.

"You never told them either?"

Zindel shook his head. Tessah spoke with finality.

"I will transport you to right outside of your town."

Erwin, Kay, and Owen nodded appreciatively.

"Zindel," Tessah cried softly, "get Dameon and Mabli home safely."

Zindel starred at his wife.

"Tessah, do you think, you could ever find it in your heart, to forgive me?"

Tessah became cold again.

"Would you be able to forgive me Zindel?"

Zindel hung his head.

"If I knew what you know, then no I would not be able to."

Tessah nodded her head and the men were gone from her sight. At that moment, Deamone came into sight. She had been listening.

"Your Highness, I think you ought to know something."

Tessah had sat upon her throne once more.

"What is it?"

"The truth of what really happened between Zindel and Tareedah."

# Chapter Forty-Six:

# A Wedding and an Execution

wen, Zindel, Kay, Erwin, Razial, and Rosemary were transported right on the outskirts of town. They could see the palace from where they stood. Zindel started at a jog in the direction of it. All followed him, however when they reached town square Zindel spotted a suspicious tall young man with a brown cloak over his face escorting a young lady with a red cloak covering her face. Zindel followed them until they were in the outskirts of town again. Suddenly the young man turned around, threw off his cloak and withdrew his sword all at the same time. It was Dameon.

"What do you want Zindel?"

Surprised that Dameon had noticed him at all Zindel stuttered slightly.

"Ju...just too...to make sure that you are Princess Mabli were all right."

Dameon replaced his sword in his holster and held out

his hand for Mabli to take it. She removed the hood on her cloak.

"We are fine good knight."

Dameon smirked at his father.

"How did you get back so quickly?"

"Your mother transported us back here to assist you with the rescue of Princess Mabli."

"Mother transported you back?! Even after you tried to steal the Golden Staff of Enchantment and give it to your King?"

"King Xavier told us that Princess Mabli would die without it. We thought we were saving her life!"

"We will see Zindel. Come Mabli."

With that, they disappeared. Zindel returned to Kay, Erwin, Owen, Razial and Rosemary.

"They are safe. They are in the Realm of the Faeries now."

Razial took Rosemary's hand.

"We are going home now. So many people will be so happy to see us."

They both walked away towards Razial's home looking lovingly into each other's eyes. A woman with brown bushy hair came running out of nowhere and jumped right into Owen's arms. She started covering his face with kisses!

"Owen! You are back! You are safe! I am so happy to see you!"

Owen was happily surprised at this welcome and kissed her right back.

"Amelia—Marry me."

She smiled a huge smile back at him and uttered only one word.

"Yes!"

Owen then put her down and faced the three on-lookers.

"Amelia, this is Kay, Erwin and Zindel. Guys, this is my Fiancé."

Erwin and Kay shook her hand with a smile. Zindel shook her hand with a question.

"When is your wedding?"

Amelia gave almost a scowl.

"Oh. I don't know…Owen?"

"We shall be married as soon as we can find a Reverend to do it."

"Nonsense, I will marry the two of you. I am also a man of the cloth."

Kay looked at Zindel with shock.

"You are full of surprises Zindel."

Owen smiled at this news.

"Kay, Erwin, be my best men. Zindel, be my Officiate. Amelia, my love, let us marry today!"

Amelia started to become fanatical for a moment.

"Marry today! But I have nothing prepared. No food to feed the guests, my hair needs to be done and I have no flowers to hold! My parents don't even know yet!"

"We shall all help cook food, your hair looks beautiful, and I will find you flowers my dear."

Amelia smiled at him.

"You will cook?"

"I will."

They all laughed and went to Amelia's parent's house to break the news and to start preparing the meal. It was a beautiful ceremony. Amelia's mother had managed to pin her hair back, she had a beautiful bouquet of flowers Zindel had managed to scrape up from the edge of Elvine Forest with Jeanie's help. Afterward everyone enjoyed a wonderful dinner and to Kay's enjoyment, ale; though he waited for everyone else to take a sip before he did. Owen told stories of his quest to his wife and in-laws with the help of Kay and Erwin. Zindel sat silently listening. A knock came at the door shortly afterwards. It was a guard with a message for Zindel.

"What is this?"

Zindel questioned not bothering to open the scroll. The guard answered.

"Order's from King Xavier."

Zindel opened and read the scroll.

"I am being summoned."

The guard waited for Zindel to come with him. Owen, Kay, and Erwin stood up to say their goodbyes. Owen went last.

"Thank you for everything Zindel."

Zindel nodded and left with the guard. When Zindel arrived at the King's throne, he was extremely banged up. He was sitting on his throne without food or drink and he is doubled over sobbing.

"King Xavier?"

He straightened up and did not even try to wipe the tears away.

"Oh! Zindel you are back! Where is the Golden Staff of Enchantment?"

"I was unable to attain it your Highness, my deepest apologies."

King Xavier's tears evaporated quickly. His anger returned.

"Mabli's health depended on that Staff! You have failed your Princess!"

"Actually, my Lord, I saw Princess Mabli when we returned to Wyveren. She looked pretty healthy to me."

King Xavier seemed stunned. He had stabbed her. He saw the blood all over her floor. Yes, she was gone when he came to, but he felt sure that she was dead.

"You had direct orders from me Zindel, to retrieve the Golden Staff of Enchantment! You have failed, so you must die!"

"Whatever your sentence shall be your Highness, but I am glad you will not succeed in your mission."

"Why is that?"

"If you were to destroy the Faeries, I would miss my wife and children terribly."

King Xavier glared at Zindel in awe for a moment. For almost sixteen years he had had a faerie right under his nose. Trusted and praised a faerie. How could he have been so stupid not to have seen the signs?

"Guards!"

He bellowed. Two guards came running into the throne room.

"Take Zindel to the dungeons. He shall be executed at dawn!"

# Chapter Forty-Seven:

## The Beheading

Almost the entire town showed up for the execution. Owen, Kay, and Erwin were in the front, as were Razial and Rosemary. They both had tear stained faces. As Zindel scanned the audience, he saw Dameon's spiky hair and Mabli's long red hair. One more scoped of the audience revealed Tessah's face. Zindel's heart skipped several beats. Did she forgive him? Or had she come to watch him die? Zindel's head was forced into the guillotine and the King himself released the blade. Zindel could hear every sound the blade made, it was moving in slow motion. Closer and closer it came to his flesh, any moment now it would tear into him and he would be no more. There was a loud clunk sound. The blade had stopped. Zindel made it stop. He pushed the blade back up to the top; he had his power's back! With a burst of power, Zindel blew the guillotine to pieces and stood up. Zindel extended his hand and the sword that was on King

Xavier's holster flew to him. Now with his own sword point at him, the King was speechless.

"This is your last breath Xavier."

The King stumbled backwards.

"You cannot kill me Zindel, I am your King."

"Wrong! I am King! I am King of the Faeries and now you will die for the attempted murder of my people!"

"Prove it!"

"I cannot prove that. It is your word against mine, but I can prove that you killed Queen Cordellia."

The townspeople gasped. Mabli stepped up to the platform.

"He also tried to kill me. He tried to smother me with a pillow in my chambers and as he was doing this he told me that my mother died because she would not strike back, just like me."

The townspeople were convinced. They started to revolt but before they could storm the execution block one of the walls of the castle was blown away by a cannon. As soon as the smoke cleared hundreds of guards dressed in gold and green were entering the premises. King Xavier shouted.

"Guards attack King Demetrious!"

His guards stood where they were and did not lift a finger to defend their King.

"Guards! Guards!"

Xavier's cries soon quieted when he realized that they were not going to help him. King Demetrious rode to the front of his men, his sword was raised.

"You have killed my Edward, Xavier."

King Demetrious' gaze fell upon Mabli. He advanced on her but his horse was stopped. Zindel was not allowing it to move. Mabli spoke.

"If it is revenge that you seek King Demetrious than killing me will spark no remorse in my father. He himself has tried to end my life. If you want the blood of the one who has spilled your own, he is there."

King Demetrious dropped from his horse and continued to advance on foot. Dameon stood in front of her; Tessah stepped in front of her son. King Demetrious slowed to a stop awed at the two pairs of wings that were fully emerged in front of his eyes. Zindel spoke.

"Take your revenge from the one who has wronged you."

Zindel pointed to the scared looking Xavier, who was showing his cowardice by trying to pull his subjects in front of him. King Demetrious did turn and go to Xavier who was now kneeling before him.

"Please Demetrious consider what you are about to…"

Demetrious swung his sword and Xavier's head rolled on the ground in the crowd. The townspeople cheered. Demetrious was amused and confused by the town's reaction to the beheading of their King. He smiled and waved at them however.

"I claim this town in the name of Stocking!"

The people cheered louder. Tessah ran to Zindel through the crowd. She finally reached him. She ran into his arms and hugged him tightly.

"I never stopped loving you Zindel."

"Nor have I stopped loving you."

Owen came up to them his own happy wife at his side.

"We should be celebrating!"

Kay came up next to him.

"I shall make a fire, a really big fire!"

Erwin came right behind both of them.

"What about a town feast tonight?"

"No rabbit!" Razial spoke suddenly. Zindel questioned Razial and Rosemary now.

"I can understand the mouse, because you are afraid of snakes right?"

Rosemary shook her head yes. Zindel turned his focus to Razial.

"Why were you transformed into a rabbit?"

Razial smiled a bit to himself.

"I knew that all of you were out there, eating three times a day and when I realized what Stella was going to do to me—I thought about one of you catching me and eating me for dinner."

Kay, Owen, Erwin, and Zindel laughed aloud at this thought. Even Razial managed to see the humor in it.

"Even still, I don't believe I will ever look at a rabbit quite the same way."

This made everyone laugh harder. Dameon stepped up to his father.

"Deamone told us what really happened Father. We tracked Tareedah down and she confirmed it. I am sorry Father. I am sorry that I shunned you."

"Do not be sorry. I never offered the truth, but trust me I am never going to lie again."

Zindel turned toward Mabli.

"I am sorry about your Father Mabli, if there was any other way…"

"He wouldn't deserve it. He was a horrible King and an even worse Father, not to mention husband. I am glad to be a part of your family now."

Zindel suddenly became upset.

"I forgot about the wedding! Have I missed it?"

Dameon took Mabli's hand.

"No, we were tracking down Tareedah and saving your neck last night."

"When will it happen?"

Mabli answered.

"Dameon and I did some thinking and we have decided to wait to get married."

"Why, I do not understand?"

Tessah came up behind Zindel.

"To give you more time being King, you lost many years being human."

Zindel laughed.

"I had years on the throne before you were born Dameon. I have been King and I am done being King. It is your turn son."

Dameon smiled at Mabli.

"Then we may be married as soon as you wish."

Upon saying those words to Dameon, he glanced through the crowd and spotted Erwin. Erwin's face looked like all the positive happy energy was drained right out of it. Zindel turned to Tessah.

"Erwin is full faerie by birth—he should not have to pay for my sins."

Tessah glanced at the longing face across the crowd.

"I suppose he does belong in the Realm of the Faeries—but the prophecy Zindel."

Zindel held up a hand to silence her.

"He wants nothing to do with the throne. He only wants to belong."

Tessah looked back at Erwin and gave him a smile, which he returned.

"As long as he really wants nothing to do with the throne, I can see no harm in it."

Zindel smiled so lovingly at his wife. Neither of them had noticed that the celebration among the town had started, for music had suddenly drifted into their ears. Zindel took Tessah's hand.

"Tessah, my dear, dance with me?"

"Of course I shall my love, of course."

# Epilogue

Velelia was sitting with Stella and Tareedah in her lair, they were chatting over a brew.

"Can you believe that Tessah allowed that Human to become one of us?"

Stella gave a stern look in Tareedah's direction.

"Excuse me…I was a human-made Faerie."

Tareedah sneered at the child.

"Yes, but you are not allowed to be queen."

Velelia spoke.

"I can't believe Goodwin consented. He has been against even the research about it."

Tareedah was pouting.

"How can they let a half breed rule over us?!"

Velelia raised an eyebrow.

"Careful Tareedah, you are the only full faerie here."

Tareedah rolled her eyes in annoyance.

"I did not mean it like that."

Stella countered her.

"Well then how did you mean it?"

Tareedah sighed.

"I do not have to answer to you child."

Stella threw her cup.

"I am no child! I may bear resemblance to one but I am more woman than you will ever be!"

Tareedah screamed and went to lunge at Stella, when suddenly she was transformed into a frog and she was starring at a fish. Velelia spoke.

"You are both behaving childishly right now. Stop fighting and start thinking! There must be something we can do."

The frog croaked and Velelia transformed them back to themselves.

"You were saying Tareedah?"

Tareedah took her seat again and glared at Stella.

"We just need a way to infiltrate the Palace right?"

Velelia nodded. Tareedah continued.

"What about Erwin, my son with Zindel."

Velelia's eyes opened wide.

"They would never let him back in. It's too close to the prophecy."

Tareedah smiled.

"Yes, I know and he so badly wants to be where he belongs."

Velelia laughed.

"We could make him a Faerie and then he would belong to us."

Tareedah smiled.

"He could challenge Dameon and his human. He would just have to pick a full faerie bride and the Ancestral Order would surely trust him more than the human-lover."

Stella magically repaired her cup.

"Too bad Dameon will already be King before Erwin is even eligible for dating."

Both Tareedah and Velelia frowned at her. Velelia spoke.

"She's right you know; besides the Ancestral Order would not see Erwin as royalty anyway. He was illegitimate by birth."

Tareedah laid her face in her hand.

"There must be something. Fate has made it so he was first born and then brought back into my life. He must play some part."

Velelia thought for a moment and then began to chuckle to herself.

"I have a plan Tareedah...I have a plan."

# Acknowledgments

I would like to thank Bradford and Colleen Baxter, my parents, for believing that I could make this happen. James and Sherry Jones, my parents-in-law, for being supportive and for being an early critic for this story. Also Johnathan Jones, my husband, for constantly pushing me to complete this project.

I would also like to thank Sarinna Crosby for being a constant guinea pig to my stories, without you Zindel and his men may have never left the King's courtyard.